*Look what people are saying
about this talented author....*

"Leto has a unique, refreshing writing style that
keeps the story moving, bringing erotic images
to new heights, while still being *romantic*."
—*The Romance Reader*

"So much sexual tension can't be healthy, but
boy, it feels good while it lasted, huh?"
—*Mrs. Giggles*

"Smart, sophisticated and sizzling
from start to finish."
—*A Romance Review*

"Leto's got the touch!"
—*RT Book Reviews*

"She loves pushing the envelope
and dances on the edge with the sizzle
and crackle of lightning."
—*The Best Reviews*

"Tense, thrilling and sexy...what more
can a reader want?"
—*Romance Reviews Today*

Dear Reader,

My family is in the manufacturing business and has been for over fifty years, but honestly, we should be party planners. Need a sit-down dinner for forty? No problem. I don't know if it's because we're Italian or just because we love to have fun, but throwing together bridal showers, surprise birthday parties and even weddings is something we relish.

I'm not sure that Leo Sharpe, one of the heroes of this collection, thought it would be so easy—especially with the ulterior motive behind his decision to throw a surprise wedding for his best friends, Coop and Bianca. Yeah, Leo's a die-hard romantic, but he's also a man with an agenda. He's wants his ex-girlfriend back in his bed and since she's Bianca's best friend, she can't avoid him while they're planning sexy, romantic nuptials!

Little does Leo know that the rest of the bridal party has also decided to take sensual advantage of this whirlwind wedding.

And to find out precisely why Bianca and Coop can't seem to make it down the aisle—and how they overcome their obstacles—check out my free short story online at eHarlequin! Links and details are up at my Web site, www.julieleto.com.

Happy reading,

Julie Leto

Julie Leto

3 SEDUCTIONS AND A WEDDING

HARLEQUIN®

TORONTO • NEW YORK • LONDON
AMSTERDAM • PARIS • SYDNEY • HAMBURG
STOCKHOLM • ATHENS • TOKYO • MILAN • MADRID
PRAGUE • WARSAW • BUDAPEST • AUCKLAND

Recycling programs
for this product may
not exist in your area.

ISBN-13: 978-0-373-79547-5

3 SEDUCTIONS AND A WEDDING

ABOUT THE AUTHOR

Over the course of her career, *New York Times* and *USA TODAY* bestselling author Julie Leto has published more than thirty-five books—all of them sexy and all of them romances at heart. She also shares a popular blog—www.plotmonkeys.com—with her best friends, Carly Phillips, Janelle Denison and Leslie Kelly. Julie is a born-and-bred Floridian homeschooling mom with a love for her family, her dachshund and supersexy stories with a guaranteed happy ending.

Books by Julie Leto

To Deb Goldman, Barbara Ross and all my wonderful friends at the Jazzercise Center. Working out every morning has become an essential component not only to my physical health, but my mental well-being. The laughs, the friendship...even the sweat...all mean the world to me.

Thank you...and let's dance!

Prologue

"MARRY ME."

Bianca Brighton threw a coy look over her shoulder and watched the man who'd just proposed dive into the water beneath the breathtaking falls at La Fortuna, deep in the Costa Rican rain forest. He swam directly toward her, his strokes powerful and measured, his body lean and muscled. When he stood, the water sluiced down his sun-kissed skin and made her totally forget his question.

"Excuse me?" she asked, still not turning to face him.

His exasperated grin nearly melted her from the inside out. She knew what he wanted. He'd asked her to marry him a thousand times before—and yet, each and every proposal acted like a major aphrodisiac. Honestly, what could possibly make a woman hotter than knowing that a guy like Cooper Rush wanted to love you for the rest of his life?

He slid his hands around her waist and tugged her tight against his chest. The cold water dripping from his hair drizzled down her shoulders, making her shiver even as her skin absorbed his intoxicating body heat.

"You heard me," he said. "Marry me."

Despite the tourists frolicking in the water around them, squealing at the beauty of the lush green plants, turquoise-blue water and massive, volcanic rocks, Bianca closed her eyes and marveled in the intimacy of Coop's arms. They'd lived together since college graduation ten years ago, but the familiarity of his touch had not lessened its potency one bit. He splayed his fingers across her middle. With his pinky finger, he toyed with her belly ring, practicing the precise flick and swirl she loved— only much lower down her body.

"Okay," she replied, sighing contentedly.

"Okay? *Okay?*" He twirled her around, hands tight on her arms, his eyes rolling with his exaggerated loss of patience. "That's the answer I get to a heartfelt marriage proposal delivered in one of the most beautiful places on Earth?"

Bianca closed the inches between them and pressed against the curve of his erection, hidden by the water from everyone but her. "Actually, when you say *Marry me,* it sounds more like an order than a question."

"So the question has been asked and answered," Coop replied, clearly having spent way too much time with her client, an attorney who needed legal documents translated from Spanish to English, which was what brought them to Central America. Bianca's career as a linguist allowed her to travel the world—which was doubly perfect because as a software designer, Coop could follow her or sometimes lead the way. They'd been to every continent except Antarctica, always together and yet never as man and wife. "And yet, I continue to ask."

"And I continue to say yes!" she said, watching her engagement ring twinkle against his tanned shoulder.

"Actually," he said, tilting his head so he could nibble on her chin, "the first time I asked, you said something like, 'Of course, now grab that zip line and let's go!'"

Laughing, she kissed him, remembering that trip they'd taken to Hawaii nearly a decade ago, when they'd gone on a treetop tour of Maui and Coop had chosen one of the most adrenaline-filled moments of her life to slip a diamond solitaire on her finger and ask her to be his wife. She'd flown across the wires hyped up on love. In the ten years since, the rush had not diminished, even if the marriage had yet to materialize. They'd applied for a marriage license so many times, the clerks of the court in their hometown knew them by sight. But she and Coop had simply been too busy exploring the world to plan the wedding of their dreams.

Well, more like their families' dreams.

"Let's get married here," he suggested.

Bianca sighed. They had, after all, had this conversation before. "Coop, our parents will kill us if we elope."

His eyes twinkled as he pulled her full against his powerful body. "I'm willing to take the risk…are you?"

Unwilling to immediately reply, Bianca pushed against his delicious pecs and threw herself backward into the water, enjoying the momentary disorientation of falling beneath the surface. In the cool, churning waters, she didn't have to deal with expectations and responsibilities. She didn't have to think about how long her mother had dreamed of Bianca wearing her vintage couture dress and how much her father had waxed poetic about walking her down the long aisle at their family's church.

Then there was Coop's family. In light of his sister Annie's not-so-recent yet unexpected divorce, the Rushes spoke of little else but the grand party they wanted to throw for Coop's trip to the altar—which they were sure, since Coop and Bianca had been inseparable for so long, would last a lifetime, as marriages were intended. Even Bianca's baby brother, Drew, had once offered to fly out to Montreal to retrieve them from an uneventful seminar if they agreed to a shotgun wedding at the courthouse immediately upon their return. Every single one of their blood relations had some suggestion for dragging Coop and Bianca into marital bliss.

Even their friends had opinions on the topic.

Jessie, Bianca's best friend since college, supported their right to elope since she hated most bridesmaid dresses. Leo, Coop's best friend since college, wanted them to pick their favorite exotic locale for a destination wedding they could all attend.

The last time Coop's boss, Ajay Singh, met up with them in Paris, he'd hinted that since his mother had no wedding to plan for him, she might jump at the chance to arrange one for his friends—if they were willing to do the deed in either London or India. And when Mallory Tedesco, Bianca's boss, had broken off her engagement to the slick automobile mogul Bianca detested, she'd forwarded every bridal book, magazine and Web site link she'd once treasured for her own.

Anyone and everyone who crossed paths with the couple seemed to know exactly how they should tie the knot, which perplexed Bianca to no end. As far as she was concerned, that rope had been twisted into an irreversible figure-of-eight since the moment they'd met. What did it matter if they had a legal document to seal the deal?

Though a ceremony would be nice.

Great clothes.

A fabulous party.

A honeymoon trip which, despite their extensive travels, they'd never forget.

Emerging from beneath the surface of the mountain pool, Bianca waylaid Coop's litany of reasons for why they should elope with a long, luxuriant kiss. Inch by inch, she maneuvered him closer to a quiet cove they'd discovered a few days ago, where none of the tourists would follow. Between the dappled sunlight, churning water, wild jungle and their insatiable passion, a quickie would be all they'd need to remind each other how little a wedding would affect their special connection.

Ten years and she was still hot for him. And vice versa. And yet, even as they glided behind an outcropping of rocks that no one seemed to know was there but them, Bianca couldn't help but wonder what might happen to the magic once they finally said "I do."

Tying the Knot

1

"YOU'VE LOST your mind."

Jessie Martinez set down her fork, a juicy olive speared on the tines, and glanced at the people around her. Annie had nearly sputtered out her beer, Drew had choked on a piece of pepperoni pizza and Ajay, who prided himself on impeccable manners, was coughing into his red-checkered paper napkin. Only Mallory continued to calmly chew her food, though when she swallowed, her gulp was audible in the sudden silence. Leo Sharpe's ridiculous proposal to throw a lavish surprise wedding for their mutual best friends in less than a week had struck all of them dumb.

Except her. She'd questioned his sanity out loud.

Leo's smile only deepened. Her ex's eyes darkened from dreamy turquoise to rich royal-blue, and his grin quirked so that the dimple on his left cheek gave her a rebellious wink. Suddenly, it was hard to remember that there were four other people squeezed into a booth in their favorite pizzeria. Or that less than two minutes ago, she'd scarfed down enough garlic salad dressing to stop a rampaging vampire.

"People have been telling me I was crazy for years," he replied, tossing an irreverent glance at Annie, who, as the potential groom's sister, knew Leo best.

Well, except for Jessie. To Coop's sister, who was six years older than her sibling, Leo was nothing more than a surrogate little brother. To Jessie, he was the man who'd broken her heart.

"And despite that," Jessie said after taking a sip of her soda, "you continue to construct harebrained schemes that accomplish nothing but inconveniencing large and diverse groups of people."

"Can you think of a better way to finally get Bianca and Coop married?" Leo asked, giving a cursory glance at the others before focusing on her. "After all these years?"

Jessie opened her mouth, but no answer came out. Though both convoluted and crazy, Leo's plan to construct and execute a wedding—complete with bridesmaids, groomsmen, clergy, guests, reception and cake—was their best bet in ensuring that Bianca and Cooper were good and wed by the weekend, the last time they'd be in the country for at least another six months to a year.

As Bianca's best friend, Jessie was ashamed that she hadn't come up with the idea. She'd witnessed the romance-novel-worthy relationship from the get-go. Bianca and Coop had somehow turned a one-night stand in college into a bond that had lasted more than a decade.

They wanted to get married. She wore the engagement ring Coop had bought from a pawn shop on the day they'd graduated from college and they renewed their application for a marriage license every time they returned to Florida to visit family and friends. But they'd never gotten around to actually walking down the aisle, always preferring to go spelunking in Turkey or climbing Mount Kilimanjaro instead.

"I think your idea is brilliant," said Ajay Singh, Cooper's boss, whose lilting accent gave Jessie a little tingle. She'd dated him once—and only once. They'd had an okay time, but while the Oxford-educated multimillionaire had treated her like a queen, they hadn't clicked. Shame, really. With his fat bank account and jade eyes, he was a hell of a great catch.

Unlike the man she had clicked with. Clicked like the detonator of a bomb.

She frowned at Ajay's enthusiasm, but couldn't maintain her negative outlook when Drew, Bianca's brother, and Annie both piped in with their support.

"A surprise wedding is perfect," Drew said. "They'll never slow down otherwise."

Annie took another long sip of her beer. "So what's next? And how do we help?"

Everyone leaned eagerly toward Leo—everyone except Jessie and Mallory Tedesco, Bianca's boss, who had never been loquacious or even social. Jessie was shocked she'd come out tonight. Leo must have dug deep into his endless supply of charm to convince her.

Poor girl didn't stand a chance. The man was lethal.

Leo pulled a scrap of paper out of his pocket, unfolded it and spread it out on the table. "I've got it all worked out."

Jessie couldn't help but glance over at his list, which was filled not only with his even-spaced, block-style hand lettering, but lines and shapes that reminded her of how he used to doodle on everything from paper tablecloths to cardboard coasters back when they were dating. Always the same shapes—boats. Masts. Bows and anchors and any paraphernalia associated with the sailing vessels he now designed and raced with great success. He'd realized all his dreams, and here he was trying to make sure his best friend, Coop, achieved the same.

He made it so hard to hate him.

Jessie sat back against the red vinyl seat and listened while her former lover outlined his plan, her gaze focused on anything and anyone but Leo. It was hard enough to share breathing space with him on the rare occasions when Bianca and Coop came to town. To sit so close to him now that she could sniff out hints of his cologne from the myriad scents in the restaurant only reminded her that while she'd gotten over his betrayal a long time ago, she had not quite gotten over him.

"There are three things that make up a successful wedding," Leo said with such authority, Jessie couldn't help but wonder when he'd become an expert on the topic. He'd never been married, that much she knew. In fact, he'd never seen anyone seriously—not, at least, since her.

"We need a quick ceremony, a great reception and a fabulous honeymoon. Your parents," Leo addressed Drew and Annie, "have agreed to take care of the ceremony. They couldn't get a church on short notice, so they opted for the main ballroom at the Hotel del Mar."

"That's a beautiful venue," Annie crooned. "It overlooks the water. It's perfect!"

Clearly, Annie was as much a romantic as Leo. Or she was just thinking about the pictures, since Annie was a photographer.

"Now, it's just up to us to plan the reception and the honeymoon."

"Won't the hotel take care of the food?" Mallory asked.

"Actually, Jessie's mom is a caterer," he said, sparing her a glance. And only a glance. Why did it suddenly matter that he'd spoken her name, but hadn't deemed her significant enough to look at? "She and Mrs. Brighton are already making arrangements. But the entertainment's not locked down—and I saw in the paper yesterday that Brock Arsenal is in town."

"The rock star?" Jessie asked. "He's not exactly a wedding singer."

Leo, once again, was not deterred. "But he does sing their song."

His voice dropped low, and unexpectedly he hummed the strains of that haunting tune in Jessie's ear. Full of sexual yearning and erotic imagery, Arsenal's signature ballad teased Jessie's consciousness, taunting her with memories she should have banished from her mind a very long time ago.

Actually, she'd thought she had.

Drew made room on the table for the waitress, who was delivering a fresh pitcher of beer. "God, Binks played that song over and over for weeks after she and Coop started dating. I thought I'd never get it out of my head. Posters of Arsenal are still up in her old bedroom."

"It would be really cool if we could get him to play," Annie agreed. "Impossible, but really cool."

Ajay nodded. "With the right amount of money, nothing is impossible."

"That's what I like to hear," Leo said, clapping Ajay on the shoulder. "I'll put you in charge of entertainment, then, okay? You and Mallory."

"Me?" the dark-haired, dark-eyed woman said with a note of protest in her voice.

"Bianca told me that you not only book all of her interpreter work, but you also find people to work with actors when they need to master an accent or learn another language in a hurry. You have to have Hollywood contacts."

Mallory remained silent, but gave a little nod.

"Good," Leo said, and then turned to Annie. "You and Bianca are about the same height and size, aren't you?"

Annie's green eyes widened. "Don't tell me you need me to pick out her wedding dress."

Leo pulled another list out of his pocket and handed it to her. "Unless you want her mother to do it?"

Jessie nearly choked, but Drew actually laughed out loud. Bianca and her mother were polar opposites when it came to fashion sense.

In unison, Annie and Jessie said, "No!"

"I should pick out her wedding dress," Jessie said. "I know her style best."

"True," Leo conceded. "But I have something better planned for you."

Before Jessie could read anything into his promise, he tapped the list he'd handed to Annie. "Think you can get all this?"

"By the weekend?" Annie asked. "No way. The boutique you want me to go to is in New York City."

Drew tilted Annie's hand so he could see the paper. It was hard to tell in the predominantly red lighting in the pizzeria, but Jessie could have sworn Annie blushed.

"That's the designer Bianca met last summer," he said.

Leo grinned. "Exactly. She said she'd totally hook Bianca up."

"I can fly Annie there," Drew offered. "I could have a plane ready by Thursday morning. We can be back by Saturday with everything my sister will need. It's about time she wore something other than faded cutoff jeans and ratty hoodies."

Jessie couldn't disagree, even if Annie did look uncomfortable with her assignment. Maybe she didn't like the idea of picking out Bianca's clothes—or maybe the idea of jetting off with Bianca's gorgeous younger brother had her a little jumpy. Annie had hardly dated since her divorce, and Drew wasn't doing a very good job hiding his obvious interest in her. He might be only twenty-six, but he was a successful businessman and an excellent pilot. Annie was in good hands.

But suddenly, Jessie did the math. If Annie went off with Drew and Mallory hooked up with Ajay, then that left...

"Oh, no," Jessie said, but no one heard her objection except Leo.

He scooted closer, his breath skimming softly against her ear. "That leaves you and me to plan the honeymoon."

She closed her eyes, trying to ignore the way his voice deepened so that the illicit possibilities in his suggestion were impossible to push from her mind. Suddenly, she imagined her body, naked and hot, pinned to the sand by Leo's muscular form with a sultry summer sun on his back and in her eyes, while his mouth did deliciously decadent things to her lips, neck and breasts.

"We can't do this," she said.

There was too much history. Too much hurt.

"It's been ten years, Jessie. Can't we let go of the past long enough to give our friends the future we could have had if I hadn't screwed up?"

Ajay picked up the bill. Drew was on his cell phone with the airport while Annie checked in with her young sons, who were visiting their father's parents. Mallory stood a few feet away, toying with her iPhone, a tiny grin curving her mouth. Leo, however, simply stared at Jessie, his pupils wide and locked on her as if she were a steak and he a starving man.

Everyone seemed excited about the prospect of pulling off the surprise wedding.

Everyone except her.

"What are you afraid of, Jessie?" Leo taunted.

"I'm not afraid of you, if that's what you're thinking," she snapped.

Leo was right. What had happened between them had been a long time ago. She'd had plenty of relationships since then. She'd been engaged. Twice, though she'd never actually made it to the planning stages of either wedding.

Over the past decade, she'd endured seeing Leo whenever Bianca and Coop came back to town. Their breakup had not affected their individual friendships with the soon-to-be bride and groom. Why couldn't she endure a weekend of travel planning with him? It wasn't as if they were jetting off to some romantic destination to check out the site for themselves.

"Then go home and pack. I'll pick you up in an hour."

"Pack? For what? If you think I'm staying at your place while we figure out where to send Bianca and Coop, you have another think—"

"I've already figured out where we're sending them," he said, scooting out of the booth, which was now empty.

Jessie didn't move. She watched Leo exchange cell phone numbers with the others as they walked to the door. Only after everyone had left did he turn around and crook his finger in beckoning.

She looked away, but she couldn't stay there all night. She was Bianca's best friend. She loved her like a sister. She'd been praying for Bianca and Coop to settle down for years, or at least long enough to make their love affair legal. The least Jessie could do was make sure that Leo didn't totally mess the long-awaited honeymoon up by sending them to kite-surf in Bora-Bora or scuba dive on the Great Barrier Reef—both of which they'd already done.

They needed something special. Something romantic.

Something that reminded them that their relationship hadn't always been about foreign travel, adventure and games.

She joined Leo at the door.

"Okay, Mr. Wedding Planner. Where exactly do you propose we send the couple who has been everywhere?"

Leo's grin was so full of self-satisfaction, she almost slapped him. Or kissed him. With Leo, the line between the two was always taut and ready to snap.

"We're going back to where it all started," Leo told her, opening the door so that the humid Florida air clashed with the air-conditioned interior of the restaurant, plunging her into just the kind of heat that normally got her into a ton of trouble. Especially around Leo.

After a split second, her brain processed what he'd said and she stopped dead, her foot stumbling on the sidewalk so that Leo had to grab her by the elbow to keep her upright. The minute their skin made contact, Jessie lost her ability to breathe. His fingers were strong, his palms warm, his forearms tan and ripped with muscles.

She swallowed thickly. "You can't mean Key West."

"Oh, yes, I do mean Key West," he promised, pulling her up so that their noses nearly touched. "In every way possible."

2

THE START FLAG had raised and the horn had sounded. Leo had calculated and planned with precision, but the operation to win Jessie back—and marry off his best friends in the process—was a risk nonetheless.

Luckily for him, Leo's gambles usually paid off. He hadn't made his way in the highly competitive world of yacht design and racing by playing things safe. Throwing off the old designs and traditions had made him a popular guy in a very elite, exclusive club. He'd even managed to keep his business afloat during tough economic times by selling his custom-made watercraft to foreign competitors who hadn't yet felt the crunch of the tight market. To attain success, he'd kept his eyes on the prize and thought outside the box.

If he wanted Jessie back, he was going to have to pull out all the stops—including those that were keeping her from admitting that she still loved him.

Okay, so he wasn't entirely certain she was still love-struck. In all honesty, his research proved the complete opposite. For three years following the swamping of their relationship, she'd refused to be in the same room with him. Until Bianca and Coop started spending more time out of the country than in, Jessie had used every excuse in the book to make sure they never breathed the same air. But when their wayward friends only had a three-hour layover between trips to Bimini or Is-tanbul, she couldn't be too choosy about which friend Coop preferred to see at the same time—and it was usually Leo.

From then on, they'd agreed—without ever speaking on the matter—to a cold but lasting truce. But every chilly "Hello, Leo" and equally icy "How are you doing?" reminded him of everything he'd lost by screwing up. He'd apologized, of course, but apparently, words weren't enough. He'd assumed that time would undo the damage he'd wrought, but even after ten years, Jessie Martinez held a grudge like a stuck anchor.

Yet the last few times they'd seen each other, he'd sensed a momentary crack in her glacial veneer. The way her eyes dilated whenever he leaned close to her. The way she didn't stiffen at his touch when he handed her a beer.

Even now, the subtle but noticeable tightening of her nipples beneath her snug blouse when he'd stopped her from taking a tumble on the sidewalk stoked him to act.

Of course, he might just be suffering from an incurable case of wishful thinking—but where was the fun in believing that?

"I'm fine," she insisted, even though he knew that if he released her, she'd likely crack her head on the concrete.

"You sure?"

She scrambled to get her feet back under her, then tugged out of his hold. She stumbled slightly, but managed to stay upright. He couldn't resist smiling. She was beautiful when she was flustered. Well, she was beautiful when she was confident, when she was shy (which wasn't often) and especially when she was pissed off. Which meant that in a little less than an hour, she was going to rival Helen of Troy, Miss America and poor, plain Angelina Jolie.

She wiped her hands on her jeans. "How are we getting to Key West? It's a long drive."

"Let me worry about transportation," he said. "The most important thing is that we get the house habitable by the weekend."

Her chin quivered. "What house?"

"The house we rented that summer," he replied. "The house on the private—"

"Island? You can't have rented it. The owner sold it."

That stopped him. How could she have possibly known?

The summer between their sophomore and junior years in college, Bianca and Coop, still in the early stages of their love affair with both each other and wanderlust, had found a spectacular five-bedroom, split-level house to rent for a month on a private key about ten nautical miles off Key West. Unfortunately, Bianca's overprotective parents had objected to their daughter shacking up with her boyfriend all alone on an island. Though over eighteen, Bianca had used her parents' concern (and threats to stop paying her tuition) to entice her best friend, Jessie, into coming along on the once-in-a-lifetime getaway.

Coop had done the same with Leo and it was on that island and in that house that Leo had fallen hopelessly and helplessly in love with the woman who now hated his guts.

Well, *hate* was a strong word. He was fairly certain that time had tempered her loathing to sheer dislike by now.

Time, however, had done absolutely nothing to alleviate his cravings for her. Yeah, he'd been the one to wreck their burgeoning relationship, but after a decade of concentrating on nothing but work and sailing, along with the occasional fling just to make sure his parts were still in working order, he was ready to reclaim the ultimate winner's cup—Jessie. He wanted her back and he was going to use this wedding as an excuse to seduce her back into his life.

"Owner listed it again a couple of years ago," he explained. "I used to sail a lot in the Keys, so a broker gave me a call."

She swallowed visibly. "You own it now?"

He smiled. "Every palm tree and grain of sand, though no one has been on the property for years."

"Why?"

Her expression was a mixture of disbelief and disgust, which on the surface wasn't a very good sign.

"I've been busy. I don't get down there much anymore and my caretaker quit last year."

"No, I mean, why did you buy it, especially if you never use it?"

"Do you really want to know the answer or would you rather go home and pack? We leave in—" he consulted his watch "—two hours."

She narrowed her eyes, searching for some clue to his motives, but finding none, she cursed and stalked toward her car. "I'm only doing this for Bianca and Coop."

He slung his hands into the pockets of his jeans. "Of course. Why else would you go with me to the remote, deserted island where we first made love?"

From the short distance between them, Leo couldn't tell whether Jessie's eyes watered on account of deep, residual hurt or blind fury. Still, his best bet was to take off now, before she could retaliate.

He slid into his convertible, rubbing his chin absently while he watched Jessie tear out of the parking lot, the backside of her car fishtailing in her haste. He hoped she made it home in one piece. Or better, that she made it through this trip without ripping his throat out. He was so wrapped up in thought, he started when Drew Brighton leaped over the passenger door and landed smoothly in the seat.

"You've lost your mind, man," Drew said.

Leo glanced at Bianca's little brother and grinned. "So you agree with Jessie that this whole surprise wedding thing is crazy?"

Drew brushed at a smear of grease on his jeans. "Nah, I agree with Ajay that the whole lark is brilliant. The only way to get those two to settle down long enough to get hitched is to totally blindside them with something spectacular. I'm talking about you and Jessie."

Leo tugged his car keys out of his pocket and shoved them into the ignition. "You don't know what you're talking about."

Drew snorted. "My sister and I are close, man. And I dated Jessie once."

"You? You're like, what? Twelve?"

Drew cursed. "I'm twenty-six and my moving company made more money than your little sailboat ventures last year and the year before, asshole, so shut the hell up about my age."

Leo mumbled an apology. He liked Drew. The kid was a few years his junior, but he'd always come across as a wise, old soul when he wasn't cussing Leo out for being a jerk.

"You're right," Leo said, lifting his hands off the steering wheel in surrender. "I didn't know you dated Jessie."

"It was just once for some charity event. We had a great time, but I'm like her brother. And I overheard enough of her conversations with my sister to know that you trashed her heart."

He nodded. "Guilty as charged."

"Then why did you set up this whole surprise wedding to try and get her back?"

"How did you know?"

Drew's gaze flicked to a minivan parked a few cars away, where Annie Rush was tossing an impressive cache of empty single-serving-size Cheerios boxes and fast-food bags bedecked with characters like Ronald McDonald and the Burger King into the garbage. "Because I like the way you think."

Leo jolted as he made the connection.

"You're hot for Annie?" Leo asked. Annie had graduated from college before Coop had even started, which put her at about thirty-eight. She had two kids and relatively moist divorce papers. Leo doubted she had the time or interest in a guy so much younger, but what the hell did he know? He'd set his future on reigniting a relationship with a woman he'd betrayed in the worst way. If the kid wanted to shoot for the stars, who was he to judge?

"Actually, yeah. Does that bother you?"

"Might piss Coop off," Leo replied. "I don't know how he'd feel about his older sister dating his much younger brother-in-law."

"I'm not interested in dating her," Drew said.

Leo held up his hand. "Look, I don't want to know. I gave you the list of stuff you need to get in New York. If there's nothing else, I've got a boat to catch."

Drew laughed. "Of course you do. I'm no expert sailor, but I've been around Jessie a lot more than you have in the last few years. Consider yourself under a severe weather warning, okay? Ten years might have gone by since you screwed her over, but she hasn't forgotten."

"Good," Leo said, revving up the engine. "If she still hurts, then she still cares."

Drew shook his head as he exited the car. "That's the best you got?"

"Better than what you got, bud," Leo said, flicking his gaze at Annie, who now looked as if she'd unpacked half of a sports equipment store out of the back of her van.

"We'll see," Drew replied. "Care to wager?"

Leo threw the car into reverse, but braked at Drew's challenge. Building boats that raced in the most prestigious competitions in the world had given him a taste for gambling. Not because he needed the winnings, but because he loved to shove his superiority into the face of his competitors. It was juvenile and arrogant, but at least he was honest about it.

"I'm not betting that you'll get into Annie's pants. She's my best friend's sister."

"Then just bet that I'll get what I want before you get what you want." Drew extended his hand.

Leo didn't hesitate. "You're on. What's the stakes?"

Drew eyed Leo's sports car, but thought better of it. "If you win, I fly you and your lady love to any destination in the continental U.S. for an uninterrupted weekend of bliss."

"Can we join the mile-high?"

"What you do in the back while I'm flying is none of my business."

"And if you win?"

Drew closed his eyes, thought hard, then smiled as if he'd

just conjured up a particularly decadent daydream. "One week-end around the Turks and Caicos on your best rig."

Leo laughed, shook the kid's hand and allowed himself a split second to imagine making love to Jessie in the sky. "You're on."

3

IF JESSIE were to select recipes to describe Bianca's family, the Brightons would have been some exotic dish that included rare Kobe beef, saffron handpicked from crocus plants in southern Spain and truffles extracted by the nosiest pigs in Piedmont, Italy. The Martinez clan, on the other hand, were more like chicken and yellow rice with black beans—exotic to people who didn't live in the tropics, but rather ordinary to everyone else. As the matriarch, Celia Martinez did not entertain wild ideas, nor did she gamble, take risks or do anything that might cause someone to get hurt. Most particularly, her daughters.

Knowing this, Jessie wasn't entirely sure how her mother would react to her announcement that in a little less than twenty minutes, she was taking off from her above-the-garage apartment adjacent to her mother's house with the man who'd once broken her heart into a million pieces. It was probably safe to confess that they planned to transform their former love nest into a honeymoon destination for their best friends—but her recently added decision to seduce Leo while they worked she'd keep to herself.

Jessie had never really been a lemons-to-lemonade kind of girl, but maybe the time had come for her to change. She was going to be stuck with Leo whether she liked it or not. The love they'd once shared had turned to bitter loathing, but as far as she could tell, their mutual attraction hadn't dissolved one iota. Her body flared with heat the minute she laid eyes on him. She'd caught herself staring at him more than once tonight—at the way he charmed the waitress with nothing more than his smile or how he savored every bite of his decadent pepperoni-and-sausage pizza as if it were the finest cuisine in the world.

Bianca's mother might have appreciated the irony and the great adventure. She might even have helped Jessie plan the ultimate act of sexual revenge. Unfortunately, Mrs. Brighton was busy planning her daughter's out-of-the-blue nuptials... and, apparently, so was Celia Martinez, who was sitting at her kitchen table, poring over her best recipes.

"Hey, Ma," Jessie said, closing the kitchen door behind her and, on automatic, heeling off her shoes and lining them up on a rack beside the refrigerator.

"Oh, Jessie! Thank God you're here. Did you hear about the wedding? Oh, of course you've heard. Alina called an hour ago. I don't know how we're going to pull this all off in less than a week? What was that...man...thinking?"

Jessie glanced at the clock. She was pretty sure her mother had wanted to use a much more colorful word to describe Leo, but in keeping with her rather strict dictates regarding proper language, she'd refrained. Still, she had a way of making the word *man* sound as if Jessie should, in a complete role reversal, demand her mother wash her mouth out with soap.

"It's the only way to get Bianca and Coop married," Jessie said. "And they deserve a cool surprise wedding planned by the people who know and love them best."

"You're right, but there is so much to do! Take these," she said, sliding a pile of recipes across the table, "and call our suppliers to make sure we have everything by tomorrow morning. I know it's late, but—"

"I can't, Ma."

Her mother's dark eyebrows knitted together. "What do you mean, *you can't?*"

"I'm the maid of honor," Jessie explained, suddenly not sure why she'd come inside to tell her mother about her trip in person. What were cell phones for, anyway? "I've got my own things to do. Or thing, anyway. But you can't do this alone. Call Deborah."

Celia shook her head, her mouth set in a stubborn moue. "Deborah has babies. She can't help at this late—"

Jessie groaned. Her older sister's "babies" were now twelve and thirteen. Deb, who'd been working for their mother's catering company just as long as Jessie, was always given a pass whenever emergencies came up—and not by choice. Despite the fact that Celia had worked full-time while her children were young, Jessie's mom had weird beliefs when it came to other working mothers. As in, they shouldn't work unless completely necessary. This meant Deb, who was undeniably more capable than Jessie, rarely got a chance to shine.

Well, Jessie hoped her sister was ready to go supernova, because not even the most skilled guilt trip from her mother was going to keep her from going to Key West with Leo.

On the drive home, she'd been angry at how he'd manipulated her into spending time alone in the very house where they'd first made love. She'd nearly driven off the road twice while contemplating how she was going to tolerate an hour on her own with him, much less almost an entire week. For the better part of the last decade, she'd either avoided him or frozen him out, trying to forget how willfully and carelessly he'd torn apart her trust.

But as she'd cruised the familiar streets of her neighborhood where she'd learned how to ride a bike, shake off a scraped knee and navigate the stormy waters of adolescence, she'd realized that she could either whine about the situation or take control. Leo's presence, if nothing else, sparked the Jessie she used to be—the girl brimming with sass and direction and desire. She could not blame Leo entirely for those qualities falling to the background, but she didn't mind giving him a bit of credit for stirring them again.

Bianca had told Jessie years ago that Leo wanted her back. She'd confided how he regretted cheating on her back in college with a girl who'd climbed into his bed one drunken night whom he'd believed—or so she'd been told—to be Jessie. Leo had never denied that he'd had sex with the girl, some tramp from his dorm who'd had her eyes on him for months. Too drunk to tell the difference had just been an extra insult she simply couldn't overcome.

Yet if Leo fancied this week as an opportunity to force their reunion, he was mistaken. They'd get "back together" only long enough to have amazing, mind-blowing sex. And this time, when she walked away, it would be on her terms and not because he balled some other girl whose name he probably didn't remember.

This surprise wedding presented her with a chance to not only make Leo pay for what he'd put her through, but also to purge the man from her system once and for all. She'd tried just about everything—she'd been bitchy to him and cold. She'd insulted him under the guise of humor and he'd always greeted her animosity or indifference with his signature roguish grin or flirtation.

He was incorrigible.

Which made him utterly irresistible.

To offset his lasting effects on her psyche and libido, she'd tried dating men who were his polar opposite—steady, staid and boring—as well as guys just like him: players with endless capacities for fun and irreverence. She'd been engaged to one of each. And yet, neither of them cleansed him from her soul.

No, she was going to have to fight fire with fire. Her plan was just as insane as his to throw a surprise wedding, but perhaps the results would turn out just as spectacular.

"Deb has been waiting for a chance like this, Ma," Jessie declared. She couldn't go off for a few days of decadence if she thought she was leaving her mother to contend with cooking dinner for two hundred people without any help. "She wants to prove she's got the stuff to take over this business when you retire."

"I'll die before I retire," her mother muttered.

"Probably, but don't you want to leave your legacy to someone at some point?"

Celia frowned. "Deb has a husband. Children. I want to leave the business to you, so you can—"

Jessie cut her mother off with a weary sigh. "Have something to occupy my lonely nights?"

Celia scooped up her recipes and shuffled the order, but without much focus. This wasn't a conversation either wanted to have again, not when they'd fought this fight so many times already. In the end, they'd simply be so angry with one another that they wouldn't speak for a week. Jessie didn't have the energy. Not when she had a seduction to look forward to instead.

Jessie knew she should have never joined the catering business in the first place. She'd done so strictly out of comfort and familiarity. Having acted as her mother's gofer for years, she appreciated the thrill of pulling off a spectacular event. But she wasn't a good cook, and her eye for design was limited to expertly recreating what someone else had put together. She'd told herself over and over that working in the family business was just a layover—a bridge until she figured out what she really wanted to do.

But that argument was hard to maintain now that she was past her thirtieth birthday.

For the first time in forever, Jessie finally had a fire in her belly. She had a goal—an attainable ambition that could lead her to bigger and better things. She hadn't realized until tonight how the memory of Leo and what he'd done to her acted like an impenetrable wall to her future life. She needed to break down that barrier, once and for all, by wiping all the "what ifs" with regard to Leo Sharpe out of her—mind, body and soul.

And if she could also give her best friend in the world the wedding of a lifetime in the process, so much the better.

"Ma, I already called Deb and she's on her way. I love working with you, but this isn't my dream. You've always known that."

"What is your dream, then?"

Jessie swallowed her reply. It was too personal for her to voice out loud. She'd only just figured out she wanted to sleep with Leo again and she wasn't ready to share her epiphany with anyone—especially not her mother.

"To throw Bianca the best wedding ever," she answered, slipping her hands onto her mother's shoulders and massaging out the tension. "She might travel the world on a whim, but she's always been there for me. For us."

Little by little, the tightness in her mother's muscles melted away. Celia had started out as a cook in her husband's Cuban restaurant, but that all changed the day Miguel Martinez unexpectedly contracted pneumonia and died. Too traumatized to reopen the restaurant, Celia had voiced the desire to do something else with the insurance money. Opening a catering business had been the top of her list, but she'd had no idea where to begin.

Luckily, Bianca's well-to-do parents had stepped in and guided Celia, helping her choose a location for her headquarters, giving her advice on how to find employees, suppliers and customers. A dinner party for twenty hosted by the Brightons had been her first gig. Pulling off this wedding was only a small token toward paying them back.

"Bianca is like my third daughter and I want her to have a magical wedding day," Celia agreed. "You do what you have to do, *mijita*."

Jessie kissed her mother's cheek and grinned when she heard her sister's car pull into the driveway. "That's what I intend to do, Ma. And then some."

4

LEO'S LUNGS tightened and then burned. Instantly, sweat stung the corners of his eyes and his hands slipped on the steering wheel of his 1969 pickup. He'd exchanged his sports car for the truck not only to carry more gear, but also to impress Jessie with its rugged coolness. But now that he'd witnessed her strutting down the stairs from her walk-up apartment in a skirt so short it might as well have been a belt, he was the one impacted to his core. He shifted in the driver's seat, his jeans suddenly snug around his package.

Great first impression, Sharpe. Greet the woman you once screwed over with a raging hard-on. That'll make her trust you again.

He glanced away, but not before he caught a naughty grin slide across her lips, painted the color of the Caribbean sunset. What did she have to smile about? Only an hour and a half ago, her fury over his plan had been undeniable. What had changed?

Her clothes, for one thing. In college, Jessie had developed a real eye for clothes that drove him wild. Never quite trashy, but always on the edge. His memory swam with images of flesh-colored fishnet hose, leather pants and a particularly tricky lace-up bustier he'd become adept at removing in ten seconds flat.

Today, her look was a bit more subdued, but just as mouth-watering. She'd paired the white skirt with a peachy halter top that made her olive skin glisten in the setting sun. Her hair, long and dark, was pulled into a messy knot that reminded him of lazy mornings in bed after a particularly hot and sweaty night. Everything about her screamed sex—and not missionary sex, either. Hot-chick-on-top sex. Suck-me-till-I'm-dry sex. Loud, grunting, never-forget-me sex.

The kind of sex they used to have as often as possible before he'd thrown it all away.

On the morning she'd discovered him hung over and in bed with some girl he hardly knew, Jessie had made it perfectly clear that she would never forgive him. For months, he'd tried everything. Flowers. Chocolate. He'd even conned his fraternity brothers into an old-fashioned serenade under her window. She hadn't even lifted the blinds.

After graduation, he'd tried just to talk to her, but despite his determination to be charming, she'd either ignored him entirely or answered every comment he'd made with sarcasm or hostility.

Only after Bianca and Coop's visits became less frequent did they call what could best be described as a grudging truce. They'd existed that way until, apparently, tonight. Because if Jessie wasn't trying to cruelly torture him with her choice of sexy clothes and flaming lip color, he couldn't imagine what she thought she was doing.

Leo met her on the cracked shell path that led from the garage to the driveway.

"You're late," she chastised, but without any of her usual annoyance. In fact, he couldn't remember the last time her voice had been so deep and smooth.

His blood supply rushed south yet again.

"Sorry," he said, dizzy. "Had to get a couple of things... together."

Without direction, his gaze dropped to her breasts, pressed up nicely by what he suspected was a dark bra, judging by the outline beneath her snug top.

He eyed her suspiciously. Better than anyone else, she knew his weaknesses. Some guys got all hot over naked tits. A few even liked those tasseled pasties that seemed all the rage in strip clubs. But to get Leo really raw, all a woman had to do was don black lace lingerie.

And the undergarments had their strongest effect when Jessie wore them.

"Are we all set, then?"

Again with the sultry voice.

"This all you're taking?" he asked, gesturing toward her single backpack.

"We're going to the Keys, right?" she asked, her face so angelic with innocence, his hackles…not to mention other parts of his anatomy…raised even higher. "It's not like I need to pack a parka."

She dropped the pack at his feet. He'd scooped it into his hands before he realized how he'd bowed down in front of her. She hadn't moved except to shift one bare leg a half inch closer to him. He took his time standing, allowing his stare to slide up her body and appreciate each and every curve.

In college, she'd been slim from a constant diet of Ramen noodles and artificially sweetened coffee with no cream. Now she had curves in all the right places, particularly around her backside, where her incredible genetics had blessed her with a booty that could make a man weep. Before he broke down, he stood and gestured her toward the truck.

"What time is our flight?" she asked.

"We have a flexible departure," he replied, opening the passenger door and helping her into the elevated vehicle. He placed her backpack at her feet and then, before he lost himself in fantasies featuring those tanned legs, slammed her door shut and jogged around to the driver's side.

"You hired a private plane?" she asked, her voice lilting with what he suspected was suppressed awe.

"Not exactly."

The truck roared to life and soon they were on the road, heading toward the marina where he berthed his favorite boat.

He hadn't yet told Jessie how they were traveling to the Keys. She'd sailed with him before and wasn't afraid of the water, but it was bad enough that he had arranged for them to be on an essentially deserted island for two days. If he added a thirty-hour sail trip with no means of easy escape, she might balk entirely.

Having not yet put on her seat belt, she scooted closer to him, scooping up his smart phone and waterproof GPS system and sliding them onto the floor. Ten years ago, he would have rejoiced at the idea of her having maximum access to his body while he was driving down the road. He could remember several crazy nights struggling to keep his vehicle on the pavement while she'd wrapped her hands around his cock and tugged him into sheer delirium.

When, for a split second, he thought he caught the same wicked gleam in her eyes, he cleared his throat, pressed down the brake as they approached a red light and said, "Seat belt?"

"You don't live on the edge anymore, Sharpe?" she asked.

He forced a confident grin. "I don't want anything to happen to you on the way to paradise. Buckle up, babycakes, or we're going to be sitting at this intersection for a while."

She pouted prettily, but did as he asked, taking her time stretching the strap across her torso so her cleavage was even more enhanced. Jessie had never been overendowed, but she always knew how to make the most of her curves.

The ride to the marina was relatively short, punctuated by her confused look when he took the exit on the interstate that led him to Harbor Island rather than continuing on to the airport. Once she realized where they were going, though, she didn't object. One moment of apparent uncertainty was followed by a quick smile and a brief "You're full of surprises."

He'd already prepped the boat for departure, so he guided her down the pier with only their backpacks slung over his shoulder. At the end was his pride and joy—a sleek, black-hulled cruiser with every imaginable luxury from a full galley to a spacious master stateroom. The weather promised calm seas all the way to the Keys, so he knew he could handle the vessel with moderate help from Jessie.

How he'd handle Jessie was something else altogether.

She stopped at the end of the dock, glancing coyly over her shoulder when he came up behind her.

"This your design?"

He didn't even attempt to contain his swell of pride. "My newest."

She leaned forward, her back arched enticingly, as she took in the clean lines and sleek surfaces of his creation. He hoped she didn't ask him any questions because at the moment, watching her backside lift toward him in unabashed offering had zapped all his knowledge about the ship. Hell, he couldn't remember his own name.

"And it's safe?" she asked, her eyes glinting with naughty delight.

He fought to restore moisture to the inside of his mouth. "Safe?"

Oh, yes. The boat was utterly seaworthy. Jessie was in no danger of drowning. He wished he could say the same for himself, because this woman—the utterly unrepentantly sexy woman, so like the one he'd fallen in love with—was pulling him under with her wild sensuality.

She quirked an eyebrow. "I'd prefer not to get too wet on our way to the Keys."

He swallowed thickly, and then regained his ability to speak. He gestured her aside, jumped onto the deck and then offered her his hand. "I can't make any promises, but I can guarantee you'll stay out of the ocean."

She smiled. Smiled! He'd just turned her statement into a potent innuendo and as a result, she'd smiled? This wasn't Jessie.

Well, actually it was. The old Jessie. The one who'd matched his wit word for word and who'd never shied away from anything exploratory in a sexual sense as long as he eased her out of her comfort zone with assurances of love that, damn it, he'd totally meant. Had all this talk about weddings and forever-afters finally softened her heart?

He made short work of the last preparations for sailing, checking the satellite radio, his navigation system and his supplies. He grabbed a life jacket from the aft compartment and went looking for Jessie. He found her sitting on the bow, her bare legs dangling over the side.

"It's a beautiful night for sailing," she said.

He handed her the jacket, which she folded behind her. "Should be calm seas."

"How long does it take to get to the Keys?"

"If we keep to about six knots, either by sail or by engine, we should be there by tomorrow night."

She glanced up at him through hooded eyelids. "And if we go…" she paused while she took an obvious visual of his crotch "…slower?"

He stepped back. "What are you up to, Jessie?"

"Up to?" Her gaze flicked back to his groin. "Shouldn't I be asking you that question?"

Again with the husky voice and bold attitude. He had half a mind to haul her to her feet and kiss the superior look off her face—so he did.

5

SHE MELDED to his chest like neoprene, hot and snug and tight. She opened her lips even before he'd pressed his mouth to hers so that their tongues instantly connected. She tasted like mint and rainwater. Her perfume, a warm scent that reminded him of the churning ocean during a sun-drenched squall, made him dizzy. When she slid her hands against his cheeks and raised herself higher to fully explore the depths of his mouth, he thought he might lose his mind.

But instead, sanity slammed into him. As lusty and raw as some of his fantasies about Jessie had been, none included her making the first move.

Even he had limits to his imagination.

He gently grabbed her waist and pushed her an inch away.

"What are you doing?" he asked, panting from the effort of fighting against what his body needed and his mind wanted to know.

"I'm kissing you," Jessie replied, equally winded. "Has it been so long that you don't remember how it's done? Because you were doing fairly well—"

"Fairly?" he asked, shocked. "Wait, that's not the point. *Why* are you kissing me?"

She sidled up closer, her pupils so round and black he could hardly spy the brown that normally surrounded them. "Don't you want me to kiss you?"

"Don't ask stupid questions."

"Then you shouldn't, either. You've got me where you want me. Why are you hesitating?"

"That's a damned good question," he conceded.

Leo charged to the back of the boat and continued his pre-launch routine until he had the engine purring, the lines released and the boat easing smoothly into the channel that would lead them through Tampa Bay and then into the open waters of the Gulf of Mexico. He was kept busy with procedures, but with Jessie's taste lingering in his mouth, he found it nearly impossible to not watch her on deck, her shoes discarded, her heels kicked up on the railing so that looking forward as he maneuvered the boat meant constant eye contact with her slender legs.

At sunset, they crossed beneath the behemoth Skyway Bridge. Glowing bright red in the dying sun, headlights sparkling like stars overhead, the structure marked the last portal into open water. In less than ten minutes, they'd be officially on their way.

But to where?

Key West was their destination, but after Jessie's little display on deck, Leo wasn't entirely certain where they were going to end up.

Her kiss had knocked his carefully constructed plan overboard. He'd meant to take things slowly and make every minute of their thirty-hour voyage count. He stocked the galley with sensual foods he knew she'd once loved—caviar and lobster and strawberries with chocolate. He'd filled the wine cooler with several tasty vintages and made sure there was lots of bottled water on hand so they didn't become dehydrated in the sun. He'd slid the silkiest sheets he could find onto the bed and filled the drawers of the master stateroom with playful items such as scarves, feathers and even an assortment of flavored massage oils. He'd expected to have to coax her into making love with him again, but after her bold and demanding kiss, he wondered if they'd run out of condoms before they reached the island.

"Everything going okay?"

Jessie came around the deck and slid her hands up a line while leaning provocatively forward.

He smirked. She was pulling out all the stops and though he didn't know why, he wasn't entirely sure he cared about her motivation as long as the outcome was the same.

"Glorious. Sunsets like this are why we live here."

"I'm kind of surprised you still do," she replied, swinging underneath the taut cords and landing on a seat near the stairs that led below deck. She braced her foot on the wheel shaft, high enough for him to see a flash of something dark between her thighs.

He shook his head, trying to dispel the image before he lost control.

"Why? I was born and raised here like you."

She shrugged. "I guess I figured you'd move to the Caribbean or Aruba or somewhere since you go there all the time to sail."

"I didn't know you kept up with my itineraries," he remarked.

She frowned, but didn't reply.

"They're great places to visit, but I wouldn't want to live anywhere but here."

"And yet you bought the house in the Keys."

He cleared his throat. "It's still Florida."

Nostalgia had gotten the best of him when the real-estate agent had called and offered him the impressive five-bedroom house after the owner passed away and his heirs had no use for a summer getaway. Leo had snapped it up. At first, he'd used the place for trials of his newest sailboat designs, but memories of his lost love affair with Jessie turned the place hollow and empty and cold. He'd moved his base of operations to St. Thomas, accepting that while he was still hopelessly in love with Jessie, he didn't need to wallow in it.

When Coop had contacted him a week ago about his and

Bianca's imminent return to the States, Leo finally had the excuse he needed to lure Jessie back to where they'd first made love.

Now here he was, headed out to sea with her on his favorite boat, and he was sweating like a virgin about to make it with the hottest girl in school.

Jessie glanced down the shadowed stairs that led below deck. "What's down there?"

"Galley. Stateroom. Head. A nice study I designed so I can work. Go explore."

Her mouth twisted while she considered his offer, but then she settled more snugly on the seat across from him. "I'd rather watch you. Manipulating that wheel makes your biceps bulge."

He couldn't help but glance at his arms, which were indeed pumped up. Most of his sail trips were not as leisurely as this one. When on land, he and his crew had to remain in tip-top shape. The rigors of international yachting competitions forced him to keep his body healthy and strong. Impressing the ladies was just a side effect.

However, if Jessie insisted on being impressed…

"You should see me with my shirt off," he countered, winking.

She raised an eyebrow.

He laughed and checked his instruments. They'd cleared the bridge. Though night was falling, he planned to remain on engine power for a while, then open up the sails for a quick run before they anchored for the evening. He could, of course, sail through the darkness, sleeping only in short intervals to arrive in Key West more quickly, but if he was going to lose Z's, he'd do it for better reasons than a faster trip.

She cleared her throat.

"What?" he asked.

"You said I should see you with your shirt off. I'm waiting."

"I was teasing."

She leaned forward and he could see her cleavage glistening

from the humid warmth of the night. "So keep teasing. I can take it. Can you?"

He narrowed his eyes, but despite the darkening skies, he could see that she wasn't kidding. Maybe she'd figured out his plan to seduce her and thought turning the tables might keep him from pushing her too far. Well, she was mistaken. He secured the wheel and tore his shirt over his head, then tossed it below.

He speared her with a challenging stare.

She whistled appreciatively.

"You didn't exaggerate," she said.

"I didn't need to."

"You never did lack self-confidence."

He chuckled. "You mean I'm an arrogant bastard."

"It's part of your charm."

"Too big of a part," he murmured. Maybe if he hadn't had such a superior big head, he might have realized that Jessie wasn't going to forgive him for slamming some chick when he and Jessie were supposed to have been in love.

"Oh, I don't know," she said, standing and winding her way behind him. "I kind of always loved your big parts."

Jessie could resist no longer. She'd tried to play it hot and cool at the same time, but the only result was a cruel and torturous tingle in places she'd forgotten existed. The lace of the thong she wore underneath her micro-mini chafed against her labia, which had swollen with undeniable want. Her fingers itched to feel Leo's skin against hers again, so without stopping herself, she spread her hands around Leo's waist and smoothed her palms against his bare belly.

"Jessie."

His voice was ragged and deep, full of both warning and surprise and surrender.

"Muscles like these can't be appreciated just by sight," she said, sidling closer. "They need to be experienced firsthand."

She pressed her breasts against his back. Her nipples instantly hardened at the contact, even through her shirt and bra.

She slid her hands up his rock-hard abs to his protruding pecs, gasping when her palms razed through his chest hair. "You didn't used to be this solid."

Despite the sound of the wind and the waves, she heard him swallow thickly.

"You would know."

"Yeah, I would," she agreed, her hands drifting down so that her thumbs flicked over his rough male nipples. "I knew your body better than I knew my own. You have a scar…" She paused while she did a tactile search for the puckered skin just slightly below his waist on the right-hand side. "Yeah, there it is."

His jeans were slung low on his hips, but to reach any farther, she'd have to unbuckle and unzip. So she did.

"Jessie," he said with a gasp.

"Shh," she insisted.

She didn't need him to hesitate. She was operating on pure adrenaline and desire, with no thoughts or rationales to stop her from touching him again. The lights from the nearby beach were shining, but the glare hardly reached them. No other boats were in the immediate area. For all intents and purposes, they were alone.

She'd embarked on this adventure in order to erase the memories of her long-ago doomed affair with Leo. He had haunted every single relationship she'd had since him. No man was quite like Leo; no lover ever made her quite as hot. She'd fallen asleep too many nights imagining what might have been if some stalker girl hadn't snuggled into his bed.

Now the games were over. She could put the question to rest, once and for all. What if she and Leo hooked up again?

The answer was obvious—they'd make love.

With a quick snap and a rasp of a zipper that rent the air like a gunshot, she had access to him in ways she hadn't for over a decade.

He was hard beneath her hand and the minute she ran a finger over the tip of his head, her sex clenched with need. Oh, to feel him inside her again. Her body wept with anticipation.

But for now, she just wanted to feel him. Make him mad with wanting.

"Jessie, you shouldn't—"

"Shouldn't what?" she asked, tugging down his jeans and boxers enough to give her room to work. "You've wanted me since the moment you saw me tonight. We're out here alone. No one to answer to. What did you used to say? There was no room for regrets on a cramped boat in the middle of the sea?"

He groaned. Maybe he remembered how he'd waxed philosophically back in the day and maybe he didn't. But she couldn't forget. No matter how hard she'd tried, even his words wouldn't go away.

She rubbed her breasts against him, invigorated by the sensation of her body against his.

"Do you know what I'm wearing underneath this skirt, Leo? Black panties. Lace. Remember the crotchless ones you gave me back in college? From Frederick's of Hollywood? We didn't make it out of the mall parking lot before you'd ripped them off."

His cock grew beneath her touch. He was so thick and hard and round. Her mouth dried. Salt from the breeze coated her lips and when she licked them, she wondered if his skin would have the same tangy flavor. Oh, she wanted to take him into her mouth, but she couldn't go too far, too fast. They had an entire trip to Key West to indulge in sensual delights they'd denied themselves for far too long. Instead of surrendering, she tightened her fingers and increased her tempo. She kissed his back and dipped her other hand lower to caress his balls.

"Yeah," he gasped. "I remember. I remember I had to rip them off you to taste you. The slit wasn't big enough for what I liked to do to you with my tongue. Licking you from stem to stern. Toggling your clit with my teeth until you—"

If she hadn't been leaning full against him, she might have stumbled. His words had conjured an instant response, and sweet fluid trickled on her inner thigh. She tugged harder and faster on his erection until he was the one exploding with hot moisture. He sagged forward, his arms hooked over the wheel.

He kept them on course with his weight while Jessie stepped back, both shocked and exhilarated by what she'd done.

And yet, before he could say anything, she dashed down below deck and found the head. She locked herself in the surprisingly tiny room, which triggered a dim, gold light. Her image in a mirror above the sink gave her a start. Even in the half light, she couldn't mistake what she saw in her eyes.

Arousal. Need. A rush she had not experienced in far too long.

She turned on the faucet, washed her hands and then splashed her neck with fresh water. The icy drops trickled down her shirt, making the stiffness of her nipples more arduous to endure. Oh, to have his tongue on her again. Inside her again.

His knock made her jump.

"Jessie?"

"I'm just cleaning up," she said, her voice pitched with nerves.

"You sure? Or are you hiding?"

She spun and opened the door, nearly knocking herself senseless in the cramped space. Not that she had much sense to begin with. Not after what she'd just started.

He'd abandoned his jeans and boxers and was standing in front of her in all his naked glory. She expected him to be lax and spent, but on the contrary, his erection stood at attention like the enduring soldier she knew it to be.

"I'm done hiding from you," she countered.

"Good," he said, taking her by the upper arm and pulling her flush to him. "Because now that I've found you, I'm not letting you go."

6

WITH ANY OTHER WOMAN, Leo might have tried to hide how he was shaking, how perspiration had begun to form above his bottom lip and how breathing came with a heavy price. But not with Jessie. He needed her to know, needed her to see—needed her to accept how she rocked him to his core.

He released her only so he could open the door to the master stateroom and gesture her inside. She headed as far to the opposite wall as she could. The cabin was spacious by nautical standards, but not so large otherwise. From across the room, he watched her suckle her bottom lip with her teeth. He should have interpreted it as a sign of her anxiety. He should back off. But damn if all he could think about was her applying those straight white biters to parts of his body.

"Shouldn't you be driving the boat or something?" she asked, crossing her arms tight across her chest.

"Yeah, I should," he conceded, grabbing a pair of swim shorts out of a drawer near the door, but not putting them on. He had a raging erection and he wanted her to understand that they weren't through. Not by a long shot. "Why don't you take a few minutes to look around? See what exactly we have at our disposal. Get comfortable. Then we'll…talk."

She tilted her chin upward before speaking, which only

emphasized her erect nipples beneath her peachy tank top. "I didn't come on this excursion to be comfortable. Or to talk."

His whole body tightened at the sound of her defiance and the flash of fire in her dark eyes. So she had thought this through and wasn't acting purely on instinct. She was attempting to turn the tables on him—and so far, she was doing a damned solid job.

"Well, that's good, then, because if comfort was what I wanted, I would have stayed as far away from you as humanly possible," he said. "Yet here I am, holed up with you on the open water and still feeling the pressure of your hand on my dick."

"Don't be crude," she admonished, but without much conviction.

He chuckled. Jessie was a lot of things, but a prude she was not.

"I'm just being honest. Maybe if you can manage the same, we'll both get exactly what we came for."

He left and shut the door behind him. He banged against the cabin wall as he hopped into his trunks, then went back up on deck. He wasn't exactly floating on air. Despite the fact that she'd given him a hand job unlike any other, his body seemed weighted with lead. Or more accurately, heavy with the power Jessie held over him after all these years.

He still wanted her. He'd devised this entire excursion on that premise. He'd had no illusions about the fact that she owned him body, mind and soul. What he hadn't expected, however, was for her to take advantage of her position of power so soon into the trip.

After releasing the wheel back to his command, he checked their location on the GPS system and corrected their course so they'd reach their destination: the relatively shallow water off a small protected island about an hour away, if he unfurled the sails. Suddenly desperate for something to do that would kill his focus on what Jessie had just done to him—and what he planned to do to her in return—he set to work. In no time, the mainsail billowed with what might seem like a soft breeze to anyone but a seasoned sailor. Soon they were listing slightly port and gliding over the water at just over six knots.

Not surprisingly, Jessie came up on deck a few minutes later. She'd wrapped herself in his yellow windbreaker and though she remained in the companionway, she tilted her head into the breeze so her hair whipped out behind her.

"I could have helped," she said.

"I needed some time."

She turned, holding her hair back while her dark eyes sought his. "I know the feeling."

"I only took ten minutes, not ten years," he shot back.

She groaned. "Are we really going to talk about this now?"

"When would be a better time, Jess? Because I've spent the last decade letting you set the timetable, allowing you to make all the rules. When you didn't want me around, I wasn't around. Then, when you had no choice but to hang out with me, I kept things cool and impersonal."

"You call flirting with me constantly 'cool and impersonal'?"

He bit the inside of his mouth, but his grin would not be squelched. "Can I help it if you're impossible to resist?"

She sighed and took the last step out of the hatch. "Apparently, so are you."

She took a turn around the deck and then settled atop the cabin roof, which was only about eight inches higher than the deck. She faced the bow and leaned back on her elbows so that all he could see of her was his bright yellow jacket, her hair flapping behind her and one bare knee drawn up to her body, taunting him with her tanned skin.

They sailed in silence until Leo reached his first planned stop, secured the sails and then dropped anchor. There were no other boats in the immediate area. The island, overgrown with mangroves and teeming with nesting birds, was off-limits and therefore wild with sound. The coastal shoreline, less than a half a mile away, was dark except for the glow of the moon against the sparkling white sand. Once Leo had the boat moored, the gentle rocking of the Gulf against the hull became soothing. He closed his eyes and allowed the water to lull him into a place of unsurpassed peace.

Until he heard Jessie unzipping his jacket.

Still sitting atop the cabin roof behind him, Jessie took her time removing the yellow material. Her skin glistened in the moonlight and, despite her natural olive skin tone, contrasted against her dark lingerie. She must have abandoned her clothes below. He ached at the lost opportunity to peel away that luscious peach top and tiny white skirt.

Not that he'd complain.

"Did you like how I stocked the boat?" he asked, his voice choked raw with lust.

She laughed and unfurled a ribbon of condoms from just inside the cup of her bra. "Kind of cocky on your part, to pack so many condoms and buy out the entire stock of the sex toy shop. Or do you have a constant supply so you can screw every girl you bring on board this boat?"

Her raunchy language didn't shock him nearly as much as what he was about to admit out loud. "I've never brought any other woman on board *The Sweetheart* before. Not unless she was on my crew. And I make it a rule to never screw any of my crew."

Still seated, Jessie leaned forward and spread her legs—not wide, so that the move was blatant and vulgar, but enough so she could lean forward on her elbows and give him a mind-spinning view of her cleavage.

"But you'll do me?"

He hadn't realized he was shaking his head until he watched her expression turn from expectation to confusion. "Do you want me to 'do you'?"

"Why do you think I'm sitting here in a black lace bra and thong? I remember what you like, Leo. I've dressed the part. I'm ready, willing and able. So let's get this over with."

"No."

"Excuse me?"

For a split second, he was just as surprised by his response as she was.

"I'm not going to have sex with you, Jessie. However, I do plan to make love to you at the first opportunity."

She snorted. "That's impossible. To 'make love,' the people involved have to actually love each other. I don't love you."

With concerted effort, he suppressed a smirk. "Are you entirely sure about that?"

She waved her hand dismissively. "I stopped loving you a long time ago. Remember? When you boned that random chick and claimed you thought she was me?"

"I did—" he shot back, but then stopped. This wasn't the time for excuses. Stirring up that nest of hornets was not what this weekend was supposed to be about. "That was a long time ago. I'm talking about here. Now."

"Okay."

She stood and walked across the deck like a Victoria's Secret runway model.

His chest clenched and blood rushed south. She glanced at the tenting material at his crotch and her smile was cat-in-the-cream.

"Hard to hide what you want in those shorts. Why don't we just get rid of them? That way, you're not fooling anyone, least of all me."

While divesting him of his shorts, she dropped to her knees in front of him. She then took her sweet time straightening up, running her hands on either side of his legs as she rose and making sure her warm breath blew across his hard, engorged flesh before she stood and arched her back so that he couldn't rip his gaze from her tantalizing breasts.

"There. Now I know you still want me and, not surprisingly, I want you, too. I mean, you've kept yourself in incredible shape," she said, appreciatively moving her fingers over his chest. "A chance to have a sexual blast from the past is too tempting to pass up."

Without wanting to, he was leaning down, his mouth watering in anticipation of tasting her again, touching her again, loving her again. His hands hovered near her waist. He was certain that if he didn't make just the right moves, he might have sex with her but he'd lose his chance of ever winning back her heart.

"And that's all you want?" he asked. "Hot sex with an old flame?"

She brushed her lace-covered breasts against his chest, a tiny moan escaping her lips before she muttered, "Essentially."

"Well, essentially," he said, grasping her upper arms and staring down into her eyes until he saw them widen with what he hoped was a mixture of alarm and excitement, "I've never stopped loving you. So why don't I just love you enough for both of us and see if I can't remind you about more than just how I can make you come?"

He didn't give her time to protest or reply, but covered her mouth with his. Sensations shot through him as her lacy underwear came into full contact with his skin. She pressed her palms against his chest, but he walked her backward until he'd draped her across the low roof of the cabin, then lowered his body onto hers and trapped her hands above her head.

For this moment, he did not want any distractions from her wandering touch. He concentrated solely on the kiss. She thrust her tongue hard against his, suckling wildly and breathing hard, but he refused to meet her frantic pace, no matter how he strained to thrust inside her.

He had at least eight hours of pleasurable opportunities until daybreak and, depending on the weather as they sailed south to Key West, more time after that to enjoy every sensual delight imaginable on a luxurious sailing vessel with the woman of his dreams. From the beginning, this trip had been planned and executed with the express purpose of reminding Jessie about how good they were together. But now he realized that the sex wouldn't be enough.

Sex between them had always been amazing. Neither of them virgins, even their first time had been mind-blowing. It was as if they'd been designed for each other. His body fit hers. Her needs jibed completely with his. Sexual compatibility had coaxed them through the rough patches of getting to know one another and as a result, they'd fallen madly in love.

So madly, he'd put the pieces in motion for ultimate destruction. He'd gone too far, too fast—and had, in circumstances he'd regret until his dying day, ruined the love of a lifetime.

His mistakes had cost him ten years of being without the woman he loved. What would it cost him this time if he repeated his actions and pushed too hard? Moved too quickly?

No, his goal for the weekend had to change. Now that she'd made it clear seduction would be no challenge, it was time to up the stakes.

It wouldn't be enough to make her come.

No, he was going to have to make her beg.

7

NEVER IN A MILLION YEARS would Jessie have thought Leo could exercise such unbreakable self-control. She was pushing him to the limits, and still he would not hurry up and get things done. She'd kissed him senseless, dragging her tongue along the ridge of his teeth the way he liked. She'd writhed her breasts against his chest until her nipples were raw beneath her lacy demi-bra. In a last-ditch effort, she wrapped her legs around his waist and mercilessly ground her sex against his.

He responded by trapping both her wrists in one hand and then grabbing her ankle from behind him and forcing open her foothold.

"Why the rush?" he asked, teasing her chin with kisses that barely touched her skin.

"Why wait?" she countered.

"Oh, I can think of several very good reasons to draw this out."

He pushed off her, but she was too winded and confused to move. Quickies had once been their specialty. With him living in the dorm and her in the sorority house, private moments had been few and far between. Half of the excitement of their relationship came from never knowing when he was going to lure her under a staircase of the business administration building or seduce her behind a pocket of trees in the horticultural lab.

Now they had all the time and privacy they could ever want and he was playing it safe?

Or maybe not. She barely had time to react when he snared her wrists in nylon line and secured it to a cleat above her head.

She tugged. She tried to sit up, but could not.

"What do you think you're doing?" she asked, forcing outrage into her voice.

He chuckled, deep and throaty and without any hint of malice. No, he was enjoying playing bondage with her and since it wasn't the first time—they'd experimented in college—she wasn't afraid. Instead, anticipation made her squirm against the bindings.

Tied, she could do no more than meet his stare boldly as he released the front hook of her bra, then peeled back the material with an appreciative groan. Though he licked his lips, he tore his gaze away and slipped his fingers into the straps of her thong and tugged it off.

He disappeared from sight while he secured first one ankle, then the second, so that she was open to him. The breeze curled around her exposed flesh, arousing her as if it were his breath. She closed her eyes and hoped he didn't keel over from a heart attack, because she couldn't move and was entirely at his mercy.

Soon after, Leo stretched out beside her. Leaning his head on his hand, he perused her body with leisurely lust.

"You're curvier now," he said, drawing a single finger up her thigh so that an eruption of gooseflesh followed his exploratory touch.

"More of me to—" She cut herself off. She almost said the word *love,* which had nothing to do with why she was here with Leo, her body trussed and her senses on alert. The smell of the salty night air was intoxicating, particularly as it mingled with Leo's musky maleness. The wind pricked her nipples to hard points, and the undulating rock of the boat evoked erotic images that could become her reality very, very soon.

His finger had reached her nipple now, and he traced lazy

circles around her areola, skimming the sensitive skin with his fingernail.

"More of you to love? Oh, yeah, Jess. And I'm going to love every inch of you. That's why I've tied you up. I won't have you grinding so hot against me I can't help but take you fast. I want this slow. I want you still. But we have to have a safe word. Do you remember what ours used to be? The only word that would make me stop?"

She didn't have to think too hard. The psychology elective they'd taken sophomore year on deviant sexual behaviors had led them to experiment with light bondage, something Jessie had never done with any other lover. At the time, they'd picked the name of their professor as the trigger that would stop any activity that made either of them uncomfortable.

The guy's name was, appropriately, Masterman. They'd laughed at the time, wondering if he'd grown up being called "Masturbate" by his boyhood chums or if he'd taken the name himself and was secretly a dominant with a harem full of submissives.

She muttered the name, but Leo clucked his tongue. "Yes, that *was* the safe word. But now, I'm going to change it. Make it more appropriate to this time and circumstance. If you want me to stop, all you have to say is 'I love you, Leo.'"

She snorted. "That's not how it works. I'm the one tied up. I'm the one who gets to pick the safe word."

"Then you should have done it before I secured the lines. Because you're at my mercy, Jessie Martinez, and I'm not going to stop until you admit the truth."

She clenched her lips together, fighting not to gasp when he nibbled her breast. The pressure of his teeth on her nipple was light, but intense. She might have bucked at the explosion of sensation, but the ropes held her fast.

"Still so sensitive," he murmured, shifting so that he was above her. He cupped one breast in his hand, torturing the tip with his thumb while he nipped at the other. He covered every inch of flesh in light, exploratory kisses and the occasional bite. He tasted every curve. Her nipples hardened, but she yearned for more than just his teeth. She wanted the suction from his mouth. She needed him to quench her unrelenting ache.

Then, with a single flick of tongue, he awakened the hot, sexual beast inside her. She gasped aloud. He rewarded her expression of pleasure with another fast lick, then surrounded her breast with his whole hand and held her still.

"Look how much you want me," he said, raising her flesh to his lips so that her dark nipple was a millimeter from his mouth. "You want me to suck you hard. I can make you come like this, remember? Remember?"

She nodded, but he didn't wait long enough to see her movement. He shifted so that he was hovering over her, his arms clenched in a still push-up above her body. His erection bobbed above her pelvis, but she couldn't move to touch her sex to his. Instead, she could only squirm while her pulse throbbed in time with the incessant sea as it slapped against the hull.

He lowered himself just enough to kiss her shoulders and neck. He took his time, exploring her body completely, exploiting her prone position so that he could linger at any spot for as long as he liked. He spent an inordinate amount of time tracing the line between her hip and her waist with his mouth, then did the same at her belly button, mimicking an in-and-out movement with his tongue that promised so much more to come.

With her knees bent over the top of the cabin and her ankles tied out of her range of vision, she lost sight of him when he moved down to appreciate the curve of her arch and the muscles in her calves. When he started on her thighs, she thought she might lose her mind. He was torturing her, learning her, taking away any power she had over her orgasm. He'd taste her when he wanted to, and not before.

Unless she goaded him. Until now, she'd been lost in the magical sensations of his pleasuring, but he was pushing her into rank frustration. He needed to do what he'd come here for. What he'd promised.

"Oh, Leo, I'm so wet. I'm dripping, like melted ice cream."

He chuckled and eased closer to the juncture between her thighs.

"Mmm," he said, his mouth nearing where she wanted him. Where she needed him.

"What flavor, I wonder?"

He slid his finger up her inner thigh, then across her moist skin.

She gasped at the sudden and brief contact.

"Oh, yeah," he said, flicking his finger over his tongue. "Nice and sweet. I'm going to have to have more of that. But not too much more. I wouldn't want to fill up."

His licks were tentative, barely grazing her labia, which continued to pulse maddeningly. When he braced his hands hard on her thighs, she knew he was going to gorge himself on her, to fill her with a feast of sensations she had not experienced in far too long. But he didn't. Instead, he took tiny sips, detailing his enjoyment and describing, in detail, everything he noticed about her body under the pressure of unfulfilled desire.

"So plump and tasty. Pink and moist," he whispered.

"You're torturing me." She struggled against the bonds, which suddenly chafed against her wrists and ankles. She could use the safe word—or in this case, the safe phrase, but to what end? It wouldn't be the truth. She could never love him again. Never.

"And you're doing the same to me, Jess. I'm so hard I think I might break. I could slide into you right now without any resistance. Or could I? Hmm, let's test my theory."

He slipped his finger inside her and at once, every nerve ending in her body flew into high alert. At his second finger, she screamed out loud. But not in orgasm. Oh, no. His touch was too slow, too lax to push her over the edge. As he intended, his unfocused touch drove her mad with want. Her heartbeat was so strong in her ears, she could barely hear him declare how she felt like hot velvet on his hand.

Then he was gone. Her breasts bobbed with her labored breathing. Despite the birdsong from the island, the whistle of the wind and the crash and flow of the waves, she heard a tiny rip of foil. She said a prayer of thanks, knowing that finally, he'd ease the ache that had built inside her so that she could hardly see.

Again, he was above her, balancing on his arms and blazing a path of kisses over her shoulders and across her neck. His erection, moist from the lubricated condom, pressed against her. She cried out, expecting him to push inside, but he only continued to kiss her until she couldn't think.

"Leo, please," she begged.

"Please what?"

"Come inside me," she replied.

"That's not the safe word."

"The safe word will make you stop."

"Right," he said. "If you say it, I'll stop teasing you, taunting you, bringing you close to the edge, but never quite pushing you over. I can do this all night, Jess. Taste you. Tempt you. Rub your nipples raw and suck on your clit until just before you come, and then stop and let the wind cool you down until I'm ready to stoke you up again. Doesn't sound so awful, actually. Sounds pretty fabulous. Maybe I'll stop—"

"No!"

He was climbing away from her, but her declaration made him pause. She wanted him inside her. Now.

"What do you say, then?"

The words caught in her throat, which had swollen with a combination of need and humility—not humiliation. Leo's little game had made her feel desirable and naughty in the most liberating way. That was what he did to her. Always. Since the beginning. Wanting her as badly as he did, he still held back. Stopped himself. Practiced a restraint she could not have exhibited if not for the ropes holding her in place.

He wanted her badly enough not to take her until she said the words.

Until she confessed.

"I love you, Leo. I love you. Now make love to me before I lose my mind."

8

MAYBE IT WAS all an illusion. Maybe it was all a lie. But high on the rush of hearing Jessie say those words, Leo didn't care. He made short work of untying her bonds and the minute he freed her ankles, she wrapped her legs around his waist and held on tight. When he released her wrists, she grabbed his cheeks, kissed him hard and pressed her pelvis against his until he had no choice but to give in.

The moment his flesh slid into hers, every minute of suffering he'd endured before now was worth the excruciating pain.

Velvety and warm, her body accepted his like a fine kid glove on chilled fingers. He pressed deep, but not hard, and in an instant, her insides clenched and spasmed around him. She cried out, and her voice skittered over the water and then was lost in the wind. Even though he tried to remain still so she could crest, the rocking boat ensured that the sensations did not stop until she'd had her full release.

But it wasn't enough. She clutched his buttocks and started to rock. Her nails bit into his flesh and tiny whimpers sounded from the back of her throat. He broke their kiss to look in her eyes, but she'd shut her lids so tightly, he thought for a moment she might be in pain.

"Jessie?"

"Don't."

He stilled, but that made her groan even louder.

"No, Leo. Don't stop. Please, don't stop."

He moved to kiss her, but she shifted her head to the side, her eyes still closed. Battling emotions rolled off her like foam atop churning waves. Need and fear. Passion and uncertainty. Challenging her now, questioning her motives or resolve, would gain him nothing. Instead, he surrendered to the basic, raw sensations pulsing through his blood. He pumped slowly at first, but then she grabbed his shoulders, lifted her bottom and met him thrust for thrust.

Moving harder and faster, he was seconds away from nirvana. She, on the other hand, wasn't nearly as close, having crested moments before. He slipped his hand between them. Barely a touch later and she was flying. He sped up his tempo until they both fell.

Leo's lungs ached. His eyes stung from heat and sweat. Despite the breeze, the night was warm—but nowhere near the incendiary temperature of the body beneath him. Bracing his hands on either side of Jessie's face, he waited until clarity returned to her dark brown eyes.

He expected to see regret. Maybe even anger.

But neither made an appearance.

Instead, her eyes were like the still surface of the ocean at daybreak, exposing none of her emotions, but reflecting all of his. The intensity made his throat clench.

"You okay?" he asked.

She nodded.

Despite the prick of cold from her sudden stillness, Leo couldn't move away. Okay, so he'd made it relatively impossible for her to *not* say that she loved him. But not utterly impossible. If she still hated him to the depths of her soul like she had when she'd first found out he'd cheated, she would not have made love with him tonight, no matter how much he tempted and tortured her. His touch had not been unwelcome and that alone had given him hope. He'd merely taken advantage of what she had not been willing to believe—that she still had feelings for him, even if the bulk of those emotions were lust and desire.

"I'm going to grab a blanket. Maybe something for us to eat," he said.

Again, she only nodded.

He dashed below deck, grabbing a cold bottle of white wine from the cooler, along with glasses, some cubed cheese, and a chenille throw he kept in his stateroom. When he returned top deck, she was still sitting atop the cabin, her legs crossed, her fingers toying with the lines he'd used to hold her still.

Her hair caught the breeze like a mainsail. The moonlight on her long, luscious neck made his mouth water. He'd just fulfilled a fantasy he'd had for ten solid years and yet, he had not had enough. Would he ever?

He set the wine and cheese down beside her, then draped the blanket over her shoulders. She snuggled into the material, then glanced up at him, her eyes still searching his. He poured them both a glass of his favorite pinot gris, which she accepted without comment.

"So," he said, a little more loudly than necessary in the stillness of the night. "How 'bout them Bears?"

She laughed, downed half her wine, then turned toward him with a smile dancing across her chocolate-brown irises. "I guess we've known each other too long for awkward moments."

"We've had nothing but awkward moments for ten years, Jess. I don't know about you, but making love to you again was the opposite of awkward. It's like nothing ever happened to end what we had."

She finished her wine and extended her glass so he could pour more. "But something did happen."

"Yeah, I was a stupid jerk."

"A stupid, drunk jerk," she amended. "Or was that part a lie? Because you always seemed pretty cognizant of the amount of alcohol you imbibed, even when you were in college. The guys almost made you the permanent designated driver."

Leo looked down at his wineglass and realized he hadn't yet taken a sip. The time had come—the confession he'd kept stored for ten years. Even when she'd first confronted him with his cheating, he hadn't told her the whole story of what had pushed him to act so out of character.

But now he had nothing to lose—and potentially everything to gain.

"I was a lightweight," he started. "One beer or glass of wine is my limit. Anything else and I get stupid. I learned that in high school."

"But that night?"

In theory, clearing the air was something he'd wanted to do for years, particularly if it meant repairing their relationship. But now, going back in time to talk about that memory struck him hard—in the heart *and* in the ego.

"I don't want to make excuses, Jess. I seriously messed up, start to finish. I was freaked out about something I'd done and went to a kegger with some guys from the dorm and drank more than I should have. The guys had to half carry me back to the dorm. Took three of them to toss me up into my loft. Must have been hours later when she climbed into bed with me. She was naked and willing, and I was still toasted. I assumed it was you."

"I never would have slept with you if you were drunk," she pointed out.

He nodded. "Yeah, had I been sober, I would have realized as much and my whole life wouldn't have imploded the next morning when you came by to pick me up for class."

She looked around, running her hand appreciatively over the sleek wood of the boat. "You've done pretty well for yourself."

"Financially, yeah. Professionally, great. But personally? There's never been anyone like you, Jess. And after ten years, I'm pretty sure there never will be."

She stood and took her wine with her to the bow of the boat. The blanket slipped off her shoulder, revealing skin that glistened in the light from the stars and moon. She was so beautiful. So irresistible. And yet, so lost.

He joined her, finally taking a mouthful of wine. The flavors of pear and almond smoothed his palate, reminding him of why he loved this particular vintage. The ability to drink great wine, travel the world and experience a thousand different pleasures came with his success as a yacht designer and captain of several cup-winning vessels. But none of it amounted to much more than a patch to cover the wound he'd inflicted on both of them the night he'd betrayed Jessie. It hadn't taken him long to figure out what he'd lost, but he'd had to spend an entire decade working out a way to heal not only his loss, but hers.

The answer had been sex. Hot, unrestrained, over-the-top sex.

But was it enough? Or did he have to go for broke?

He'd taken a step toward the stairwell when she said, "I think you may have romanticized our relationship, Leo."

"Hard not to," he replied, his attention diverted from the evidence he'd kept of his love for her. He'd carried the box with him ever since that morning—ever since he'd allowed his fear of a committed future to cloud his judgment. "It was a romantic time."

"But it wasn't real," she insisted. "It was all hormones and freedom and exploration. We were kids. And the minute things got hard, we were done."

He couldn't deny that they were young. Too young. And yet, their age hadn't kept him from doing something that had scared the crap out of him so much at the time, he'd gone out drinking and ruined his future.

"You were done," he said. "I was never done loving you. If you would have let me back in—" he started, but she speared him with a weary look that stopped him.

"What kind of idiot would I have looked like if I'd forgiven you?"

"Looked like to whom? I only cared about you."

"And I care—cared—about you. I loved you, Leo."

He raised an eyebrow, hoping an injection of humor might dispel some of the sorrow muddying her eyes. "Just a while ago, you claimed to still love me, or was that just something you said so I'd finish what I started?"

She glanced down, but he hooked his finger beneath her chin and lifted her face to his. Finally, he spied emotion within the stormy, decadent depths of her irises. If he could get her to tell him the truth, to dig deep within herself, he'd know what to do next.

"Tell me, Jessie. Which was it?"

She closed her eyes, but only for a moment. When her gaze met his this time, the confusion and pain there nearly cracked his chest.

"Honestly, I'm not sure anymore. And I'm not sure I'll ever figure it out."

9

THE CONFESSION exhausted Jessie's entire store of strength. When she'd agreed to this excursion with Leo, she'd been sure of herself, determined to have wild, hot sex with her ex and then leave him behind once Bianca had thrown her bouquet. But now, only hours into their trip to the Keys, she'd lost her resolve.

He'd made her say, "I love you, Leo." Out loud. And as much as she'd like to think she'd only complied in order to give her body the release she'd so desperately needed, she suspected otherwise. The phrase had sounded natural. Liberating. The uplifted sensation in her heart that had immediately followed her declaration couldn't be denied. She'd been suppressing the sentiment like a devastating secret. Even from herself.

Had she meant it? Did she still love Leo? After all he'd put her through? She did not know the answer, but until she did, she'd never move on from the relationship she'd thought had ended years ago.

Leo accepted her decision to go below deck with no argument. She showered in the cramped head, dried off with towels that smelled like sunshine and sea salt, then climbed into his bed. Planning for a weekend of sex, she had not packed any pajamas and wasn't entirely comfortable rummaging through Leo's drawers again. When she'd explored the cabin earlier, finding all the sexy toys he'd brought on board had been funny. Exciting. Intriguing. They'd always been fearless in their sexual pursuits and Jessie had never found that comfort level with any other man.

However, right this minute, she didn't want to think about sex—especially when Leo was above deck, still sweaty from their lovemaking and probably, knowing Leo, not entirely satisfied. Yes, their bondage game had resulted in the most explosive orgasm she'd had in years, but good sex always made Leo want more sex. And while she'd always loved that about him, she couldn't help wondering if his insatiable quality had contributed to his cheating.

Though she burrowed beneath the comforter and the chenille blanket, she never warmed enough to sleep deeply. She drifted between remembering how he'd brought her to sexual heights she hadn't scaled in years and experiencing a nightmarish replay of the morning she'd discovered him in bed with another woman.

Jessie's subconscious couldn't conjure a single detail about the woman she'd found him with. Not her hair color, her height or even her build.

She wasn't important.

Leo was what was important.

Their past made her who she was—a woman who'd been wandering for way too long and who did not trust the men whose lives intersected with hers. Her father had died so young. Leo had betrayed her in the cruelest way.

And yet, she had to forgive him. If she didn't, she'd never move on.

She was dreaming about swimming upward, pushing through the currents of the deepest, darkest depths of the ocean when the bed sagged beside her from Leo's weight. She was immediately aware that he was as naked as she was, but his body brought warmth to the shivers she'd suffered throughout the night.

"You're like ice," he said, immediately spooning his body against hers.

"Maybe I should have brought that parka," she joked, her teeth chattering.

"Maybe you just need me."

"Yeah," she confessed, shifting her bottom so that his semi-hard sex nestled between her cheeks. "Maybe I do."

For a split second, his muscles tensed, but she relaxed into his warmth until his tight reaction melted away. Little by little, his heat transferred into her. He ran his hands up and down her arms, creating a friction that first only brought her comfort and warmth, but then ignited her senses. The scents of the Gulf clung to him—the salted breeze surrounded him like another layer of skin.

"Where are we?" she asked.

"Heaven," he replied, gently kissing the back of her neck.

She couldn't contain her laughter. "I didn't know Heaven was off the coast of west central Florida."

"Mmm," he confirmed, his lips buzzing against the skin just above her collarbone. "Heaven is wherever you are, Jess."

As he nuzzled, his sex grew harder and longer. The intimate transformation against her body made her quiver.

"You always have the right words," she said.

"Not always."

His tone dipped low with regret and Jessie turned around. Now, his erection curved against her stomach, the head pressed tight to her belly button. She tried to ignore the thick length of him long enough to say what she had to say.

She stared into his ocean-hued eyes and willed herself not to get lost in their flecks of azure, turquoise and sapphire.

"Sometimes you said all the right words, but I wasn't ready to hear them."

"Like when I said, 'I'm sorry for betraying you'."

A reluctant smile teased the corners of her mouth. "Yeah, like then."

"Are you ready to hear it now?"

Without consciously deciding to do it, she lifted her hand to his face. His cheeks, rough with stubble, felt like silk beneath her touch. His lips, slightly cracked from the wind, quaked beneath her exploring thumb as he inhaled and exhaled with increasing heaviness. When she finally mustered the fortitude to look into his eyes again, she lost her ability to breathe.

He loved her so deeply. So completely. She could see the emotion in his eyes as clearly as she could see the ocean floor in a crystal-blue Caribbean sea. But she could not base her decision on his eyes. His every action over the past ten years, his every word and joke and traded barb had declared how his feelings for her had not changed, despite his one transgression—a transgression she still did not understand.

"Leo, what did you do to make you want to get drunk that night?"

He squeezed his eyes shut, then rolled away from her. She started to protest, but he flipped on a reading light, opened a drawer beside the bed and took out a long wooden box, like the kind her father used to have to hold spare change and shirt stays and the tie clips he never wore.

But there was none of that detritus inside Leo's box. There was nothing but a second box, battered and dented in a corner, but unmistakably covered in cheap, red velvet.

Her breath froze. She stared at him, disbelieving, but he inhaled deeply and pressed on. The box opened with a squeak and inside was a diamond solitaire ring with barely a chip of the precious stone in the center.

"I bought this," he confessed. "I was going to ask you to marry me."

Jessie covered her mouth with her hand, willing her emotions in check. She'd been proposed to twice before, but never like this—never with a ring chosen by a man who loved her so completely.

"How did you afford it?"

"Well, it wasn't worth much," he confessed.

She laughed, but only for a second. "But back then—"

"My dad gave me some cash for a new car, since mine was always conking out when I needed to get to work. But do you remember that weekend before? When you got a job house-sitting for that professor your mother knew."

God, how could Jessie have forgotten? She and Leo had played house for three days straight, cooking meals together, reading magazines by the pool and making love in just about every private space available indoors and out. They'd been wild, reckless and insane.

But crazy enough to propose marriage when they were both barely in their twenties and still in school?

"You used the money to buy a ring? For me?"

He nodded, but his nostalgic smile offset the look in his eyes that confirmed how out of his mind he'd been.

"I just wanted to be with you for the rest of my life. I went to that pawn shop on 56th Street and found this, but my car broke down a block away from campus and I realized I hadn't thought the decision through. I wanted to be married to you, but I was supposed to be young and free and a twenty-year-old college guy who went to parties and—"

"Drank too much," she filled in.

He nodded. "Jess, I love you. That never changed, not for an instant. I was a stupid idiot. It's my fault everything fell apart and I—"

She silenced him with three fingers over his amazing, sexy lips. "You don't need to apologize anymore."

Her emotions attempted to choke her, but she held them back. All except forgiveness. And acceptance. And, because it snuck in at the last minute—regret.

"But I am sorry, Jess," he insisted. "I can never make up for how I hurt you."

She forced a smile in an attempt to waylay the tears stinging her eyes. "You could try."

He didn't laugh, but instead ran his hand through her hair, curving the strands away from her cheeks and forehead, as if he needed to see absolutely every part of her face to gauge if she was telling the truth.

"You're sure?"

"No ropes necessary this time," she whispered. "Just make love with me, Leo. Real love."

"Okay," he said, faking reluctance until she smacked him lightly on the shoulder. "But first, you have to wear this."

The years had filled out her fingers so that the tiny gold band with the sparkly chip in the center only fit around her pinky, but tears still spilled from her eyes as he slid the ring onto her hand. He asked no questions; she gave no answers. There was nothing left to say.

He curved his fingers around her chin and lifted her mouth to his. He barely touched her lips the first time, but in slow degrees, with a succession of nips and tastes, turned the kiss into something wonderful and intimate and new, as if they hadn't just had sex a few hours ago, as if they'd somehow gone back in time to the moment so long ago on that private Key West island when they'd frolicked in the ocean, splashing and teasing and taunting until the sexual tension erupted into a passion that had burned so hot, it had scarred them both.

But while this kiss evoked the past, it was also nervous, awkward and untried. Jessie learned his mouth all over again. They bumped noses twice. But after concentrating and exploring and practicing for what seemed like hours but was likely only a few minutes, they discovered a rhythm that drew them together like the waves and the sand.

Not the rhythm from the past, but a new song, a new beat, a new experience.

A new love.

Jessie found her hands not wanting to leave his chest, where she could feel his heartbeat thudding through his warm muscles. She kissed her way across his torso, loving the taste of his skin, reveling in the way her mouth and tongue made him weak with wanting. Soon, he was beneath her, surrendered and compliant, allowing her full access to every part of him, which she took with outright greed.

His nipples were short and tight in her mouth. His hot skin scorched her tongue as she descended his body. The musky scent of his sex made her dizzy. She lazily licked the full length of him, emboldened by his groans of pleasure and frustration.

She flicked her tongue across the tip of his head, tasting a salty pearl and knowing he was utterly under her control.

When she took him completely into her mouth, it broke the last of their reserve. She sucked him hard, caressing his balls and stroking his length until he grumbled her name in a tone that reminded her of thunder. Seconds later, his hands were on her, caressing her breasts, plucking her nipples and tearing through her hair with such abandon, she knew he was close to the edge. But she didn't want him to come anywhere but inside her. She slowed her tempo to slow, languorous licks.

"Jessie," he beckoned.

She kissed her way up his body, landing last on his lips, which she nipped with as much gentle adoration as he had given her. He fumbled beneath her to reach the bedside drawer again. This time he withdrew protection, which she took from him.

Once sheathed, he grasped her hips and moved to twist her beneath him. She stopped him with a hand to his chest.

"Oh, no," she said, her voice brimming with promise. "This is my show this time." She leaned forward and undulated her hips until her natural moistness met the lubricated tip of his erection. "Now, tell me you love me."

"You know I do," he said, his words sharp and staccato as he drew in unsteady breaths.

"I want to hear the words, Leo. More than I ever wanted to hear your apology, I want to hear how you—"

"God, Jess," he interrupted, his hands adoring her body while his eyes made mad, passionate love to her soul. "I love you. I love you more than any words could ever express. I love you more than…"

She tilted her hips so that she slid onto him and the rest of his sentiment was lost in a maelstrom of sensations that silenced them both.

10

"You lose," Leo said shortly after his cell phone rang before dawn on Thursday morning and his caller ID identified the person on the other end as Drew Brighton.

Okay, so it was bad form to brag, and probably even a worse transgression to kiss and tell, but he figured that Jessie wouldn't mind. It wasn't like the whole world wasn't going to know of their reunion in less than twenty-four hours once they returned to Tampa and broke the news to Cooper and Bianca that not only had their best friends planned a surprise wedding for them, they'd also kissed and made up.

And then some.

They'd woken early to share the sunrise, having finished prepping the house for the honeymoon in record time—which wasn't unexpected, since Leo had hired a team to come in the week before and do all the heavy lifting. All he and Jessie had to do was stock the fridge with delicacies such as champagne and caviar, replace the dusty cotton sheets in the master suite with silk ones (which they also did in the guest room, much to their own enjoyment) and transfer a few of the unused sexual aids they'd brought on the boat into the master suite.

Not that much was left. Some massage oil. A few ticklish feathers. A pair of cushioned handcuffs. Child's play compared to the games he and Jessie had been enjoying in between sailing and preparing for the wedding, making up for lost time.

"I don't believe you," Drew said.

"Here." Leo handed the phone to Jessie, who'd been standing behind him, her arms wrapped around his waist impatiently, since Drew's call had interrupted what was going to be a very leisurely dinner of freshly caught lobster, followed by a second round of Truth or Dare, after the first had been interrupted last night when the dares became much more interesting than any truths.

"Hey, Drew," she answered. "You should know better than to bet against a guy like Leo. I learned that lesson the hard way. Well, not so hard. Unless you consider his—"

She laughed when Drew's objection to the direction of her sentence echoed loudly over the phone.

Leo chuckled along with her, never imagining that he could be this happy. Yeah, he'd come into this venture to win Jessie back with a boatload of confidence, but even winners took a tick in the *L* column every so often. Luckily for him, Jessie had proved not so much an opponent as a teammate. Working with her, whether it was on adjusting the sails to lean them more heavily into the wind or deciding which scented candles their best friends would enjoy the most in the large master bath with the whirlpool tub, they'd bickered without malice, compromised with ease and made love until they could barely stand.

After only a few days, their decade apart had seemed like minutes. Or perhaps, like a horrible dream. Even now, as Jess chatted with Bianca's brother on the cell phone, he had trouble keeping his hands off her. His palms itched to touch her. His ears ached to hear those tiny moans of pleasure and satisfaction that let him know she was seconds away from an orgasm. His heartbeat intensified at the sound of her laughter or the gentle sniffles that accompanied her tears.

"Yes, I know all about your little bet," Jessie said, sliding her free hand over Leo's cheek while he tried to decide if nibbling on her neck while she was on the phone was a punishable offense. And if so, which was the best punishment for him to choose? "Leo told me everything. Including how you plan to seduce Annie Rush. You do realize that she's—"

Apparently, Drew cut her off. Leo knew the kid didn't care how much older Annie was or that she had two children or that she was the sister of the man who was about to marry into his family. Leo appreciated Drew's determination to not only beat the odds, but everyone's expectations that he'd fail. Leo had been there, done that and come home with the cup.

"Yeah, I was thinking about a trip to Las Vegas, actually," Jessie crooned. "Who better to go with than Leo, a man who has an incredible capacity for sin?"

Her voice fairly purred and Leo grabbed for the phone. He was rewarded for taking the conversation out of her hands by her unbuttoning his shirt and smoothing her now free fingers over his chest.

Leo cleared his throat and attempted to end his call to Drew as quickly as possible.

"This wasn't a fair competition," Drew complained.

"All's fair in love and war," Leo quoted.

"Yeah, but Annie and I haven't even left for New York yet."

"Well, Jessie says she wants to go to Vegas and right now, I'm not in the mood to deny her anything."

He didn't know if Drew could hear her wicked giggle, but as her fingers deftly worked the top of his jeans, Leo didn't much care.

"Okay, then let's amend the bet," Drew proposed. "Give me a chance to get back in the game. If I've got Annie on my arm once we arrive back in Tampa, you get your flight to Vegas and I get my trip to Turks and Caicos."

Jessie tugged down Leo's jeans and was toying wickedly with the top of his boxers.

"Yeah, yeah. Whatever you want," Leo said, his voice cracking before he added, "Good luck," and ended the call.

Jessie splayed her hands on his chest, running them down his abdomen, then back up to his shoulders. "You didn't just agree to extend your bet with Drew, did you? You shouldn't bet against Annie."

Leo tossed his phone aside and divested Jessie of the top of her bikini. Once he had her breasts buoyed in his hands and the curve of her neck at the mercy of his mouth, he couldn't have cared less about anyone else's romantic relationship. But at the same time, he was on the top of the world. Why shouldn't Annie and Drew find the same ecstasy if that was what was in the cards?

"I'm not betting against Annie," he murmured against her skin. "I'm betting on love."

She speared her hands through his hair. "I'd forgotten how romantic you are."

"Then why don't we find a comfortable spot somewhere in this huge house and I'll spend the rest of the day reminding you?"

Take This Man

_1_

ANNIE SWALLOWED HARD, trying not to salivate as Drew Brighton strode toward her from across the parking lot. Suddenly, the private airfield where they'd arranged to meet seemed tightly enclosed rather than wide-open to the sky. Dawn was at least a half an hour away but the light standing sentinel above her van illuminated him just enough to make her insides flutter. Long, sandy-brown hair. Perfect shoulders. Cocky stride. And his face—if she'd known him back when she was taking pictures for a living, she could have switched to fashion photography and made a mint off his cheekbones alone.

Hell, with his lips and fawn-colored eyes, she could have bought a Cessna aircraft like the one sitting on the other side of the hangar. Sleek and modern and powered by twin jet engines, she'd spied their ride on her way into the airport and she couldn't help but compare the man to the machine. Both were powerful and more than likely, both were fast. But where the aircraft wore its skin taut to its frame, Drew preferred a leisurely mode of dress. His shirt, a loose-fitting cotton button-down with dark green alligators on off-white fabric, only hinted at the musculature underneath—pecs, abs, delts and obliques that she'd memorized just over a year ago when the company he owned, the appropriately named Hunks With A Truck, had transported all her worldly possessions from Jacksonville to Tampa.

At the time, watching him tote one end of her peanut-butter-and-jelly-stained couch, shirtless and sweaty, had made her feel like one of those desperate "cougars" she'd read about in women's magazines.

Now, with the next forty-eight hours free of all encumbrances and responsibilities except to make sure that her future sister-in-law looked gorgeous on her wedding day and irresistible on her wedding night, the memory made Annie want to growl. And possibly pounce.

But those instincts weren't going to hasten them to New York City and Annie, who hadn't been north of the Mason-Dixon Line in eight years, couldn't wait to get into the air. She tamped down her suddenly reignited libido and gave Drew her sweetest smile.

Unfortunately, he only had eyes for her luggage.

"You know," he said, pushing his long hair out of his eyes with the kind of casual grace only a man in his twenties could master, "I might make a living as a mover, but I was kinda hoping to get this week off."

She looked at her baggage and tried to remember the days when she could survive weeks in Thailand on a single pair of jeans, two T-shirts and a thong.

"I didn't know what I'd need," she said. "So I guess I just brought everything."

He gave the largest bag an exploratory lift.

"Got your driver's license in this thing?" he asked.

"No, it's in my purse," she said, indicating the massive leather tote that, a long time ago, had been her favorite camera bag. And after that, a diaper bag. Now, it was an all-purpose carrier of everything from water bottles to chewing gum to a confiscated slingshot and a half-eaten bag of Doritos.

"And your favorite lip gloss?" he continued.

"Excuse me?"

"I have a sister, which means I know that no self-respecting woman goes anywhere without her favorite lip gloss," he explained with a full-on, melt-your-insides smile that must have been lethal to girls his age. It was doing amazing things to her and she was old enough to be…well, his older sister. Maybe even his cool aunt.

She tried to quell a chuckle, but failed. She did indeed have a favorite gloss. It was a boring shade of taupe, but had just enough gold sparkle mixed in to make her feel pretty when she most needed it and a faint chocolate flavor that made it worth the trouble of application.

"Also in the purse," she replied.

"I sense a pattern."

He picked up her smallest suitcase.

"Personal items," she said before he asked.

He nodded, slung the overnight bag onto his shoulder, then tossed her big bag filled with jeans, sweaters, a couple of pairs of pants and one nice blouse, in addition to pajamas, a selection of snacks and extra antibacterial wipes into her minivan and slammed the door shut.

"Hey!" she protested.

He fished her keys out of her purse and pressed the lock function. "Did you really need all that stuff, or are you just so accustomed to not going anywhere without the entire contents of Walmart that you did it on reflex?"

She opened her mouth to deny his accusation, but shut it promptly. He was right. The motto of the Boy Scouts might be *Be Prepared,* but she was fairly certain it had been coined by the first Boy Scout's mother.

"What about my clothes?"

A gleam flashed across his intoxicating champagne-colored eyes that, in anyone else, Annie might have thought implied that she wouldn't need any clothes for the next two days. But this was Drew. Bianca's brother. Bianca's *younger* brother.

She simply was not that lucky.

"Aren't we going to New York to shop?" he asked.

"I meant clothes for *me,*" Annie replied. "We're filling Bianca's trousseau in Manhattan, not mine."

"Who says?" he asked.

"My bank statement," she replied.

He waved her off. "Let's not worry about details. I was supposed to spend this weekend on a gambling junket. Saved the money from the last time I left Vegas with a profit. Instead, we'll have fun in New York. And if that includes picking up a couple of things for you, that's cool. Now, let's move. I want to be in the air before sunup."

Drew started toward the tarmac, nothing if not decisive. Only a year ago, he'd taken what could have been the most chaotic time in her life—the emotional and gut-wrenching move out of her marital home—and turned it into just a blip on the radar that was her life. He'd directed every aspect of packing up her world, from the porcelain doll she'd found in a Dresden antique shop to the complete set of *Cars* toys her sons had collected from McDonald's. He'd kept her boys occupied with little jobs like counting boxes or filling cartons with foam peanuts while she'd spent a day and half surreptitiously ogling some of the hottest guys she'd seen since the summer she'd spent as team photographer for the Brazilian *futbol* league.

Without Drew, the move might have spun into a maelstrom, not only for her, but for her children. Only five and seven at the time, Will and Andy hadn't understood why they had to leave their Thomas the Tank Engine bedroom behind or why they were leaving town when their daddy was on yet another business trip. Wouldn't he be mad when he came home and found the house empty? How would he know how to find them?

Her boys had no way of knowing that their father probably wouldn't notice they were gone. Devoted to nothing but his job, her ex worked eighty hours a week—and that was during Christmas. She and the boys had been reduced to photographs he kept on his desk to impress clients.

The divorce had been quick and decisive—but thanks to a fit of raging guilt, her ex had been generous with child support and alimony. She'd always been frugal, but she could afford to spend a little on herself. Just this once.

The last new thing she'd bought for herself was the T-shirt she was wearing—a bright purple, form-fitting number that hugged her curves and made her boobs look much perkier than they actually were.

In fact, her whole body felt a lot livelier since Drew showed up.

Drew led her through a hangar. In addition to several other planes, she spotted his sleek red convertible. As he snagged a battered leather duffel from the passenger seat before motioning her to follow him out the large double doors at the other end of the building, she recalled tooling around in a similar car the year she'd spent in France, Italy and Spain with a ne'er-do-well author who'd hired her to shoot the images for his book on the origins of the kiss.

The publication had been a boon to her career, and the affair she'd had with the author hadn't been so awful, either. Yet again, she was reminded about how drastically her life had changed in the past decade. She'd put her career aside to raise her boys and as for affairs, she hadn't had one of those since she'd met her ex-husband.

But this wasn't the time for regrets. The next three days were about Coop and Bianca and their incredible journey to matrimony which, hopefully, would turn out better than her trip down the aisle. Unlike her, her brother had found precisely the right woman.

Leo's suggestion that they plan and execute a surprise wedding for Cooper and Bianca couldn't have come at a better moment. Her ex's parents, recently retired to the other coast, had her sons for the entire week. Though she'd arranged for them to return early to attend their uncle's wedding, this was the longest she'd been without her children in almost nine years.

And as much as it went against every motherly instinct she'd acquired, she deserved a little fun.

Maybe a lot of fun, she thought as Drew leaned out of the plane and extended his hand to help her up the stairs. Her insides might have actually liquefied at his chivalry if she didn't know that he was just being polite.

Well, maybe her insides melted a bit anyway, especially when she registered how nice his callused palms and long fingers felt against her skin. She wasn't used to an adult male showing her any attention, even for the sake of manners. Most guys caught sight of her flanked on either side by her punks— known to everyone else as her adorable sons—and ran for the hills.

But Drew had liked the boys.

Probably because there wasn't that much of an age difference.

Okay, that wasn't fair. Drew wasn't a boy. No, there was nothing boyish about him—except maybe that smile.

She followed him into the cockpit, watching with awe as he went through the flight checklist with rapid efficiency. He gestured for her to take the copilot's seat and once she was buckled in and wearing the lightweight headphones he handed her, she found it a lot easier to forget she was a single mom with four loads of dirty laundry waiting for her at home. For the first time in years, she experienced that old, forgotten thrill she'd get from an exciting assignment in some unexplored or dangerous corner of the world.

Takeoff occurred without a hitch. Drew's ease while responding to the command tower waylaid any fears she might have had, along with the way he flicked, pressed and manipulated the controls to the plane with total confidence. She'd just started to relax when music suddenly blasted in her ears.

He turned down the volume before she could identify the song, though if it hadn't been released more than ten years ago or didn't play on Radio Disney, she was pretty sure she wouldn't have heard it before.

"Sorry. I like it loud once I'm at cruising altitude," he explained.

"'s okay," she said, willing her heartbeat to normalize. "Loud music and I are old friends, though for licks that loud, I used to go to live performances."

"Don't tell me you were a groupie back in the—"

He stopped himself, but the sentiment hung in the air like pea soup–thick fog in London.

"Day?" she supplied. "Like the dark ages? Yeah, those mandolins and pianofortes were hell on the eardrums."

"I didn't mean it that way," he said.

She reached over the console and patted his hand. She'd fully intended the physical contact to come across as motherly, but any thoughts of June Cleaver disappeared the minute her flesh made contact with his. No, her thoughts went straight to Demi Moore. She was a mother, wasn't she? Had a whole passel of kids.

And she had Ashton Kutcher, too.

A much-younger-than-her Ashton Kutcher. At least he was over thirty, while Annie was sure Drew was only about twenty-six. Of course, Annie wasn't exactly in her forties, either, while gorgeous Demi had passed that milestone a while back. Annie still had a couple of years left until she hit the big four-oh.

But not many—which made her wonder if the time had come for her to start making those years count.

So instead of shying away from the sizzle of sensation vibrating from his skin to hers, she surrendered to it, leaving her hand atop his, hoping he'd realize the contact was no longer meant to be conciliatory or even friendly.

It was an invitation. Would he accept?

A split second later, his fingers shifted. Her lungs seized at the thought of him pulling away, but instead, he turned his hand so that his was now possessively on top of hers.

2

AFTER THEY'D MAINTAINED cruising altitude and speed for ten minutes and received an all-clear from the nearest tower, Drew set the instruments to autopilot, removed his headphones and watched Annie stare out the windshield to the east, her hand still on the center console. He'd held it for barely a minute before navigating the plane took precedence, yet the soft, warm feel of her skin beneath his still thrummed like an echo against his flesh—an echo of a sensation so powerful, he simply had to feel it again.

This time, when he brushed his fingers over hers, she turned with a start.

God, she was beautiful. Her irises, wide with surprise, sparkled like the emerald-green waters of the Gulf against pale white sands. Her hair, recently dyed red and styled in a sassy bob, contrasted with the anxiety quaking through her. She moved to tug her hand from his, but he held steady. The translucent skin at the corners of her lashes crinkled as she forced a smile.

"Small planes make me nervous," she said, as if trying to explain her reason for holding his hand before, but clearly not wanting to now.

"No, they don't," he contradicted. "You used to fly all over the world in planes a lot less luxurious and reliable than this one."

"How do you know that?"

"I know all about you," he assured her, then decided he was going to sound like a stalker if he didn't clarify where he got his information. "Bianca talks about you all the time."

Her free hand flew to her heart as if she were hugely relieved. "Bianca's sweet. And she's good for my brother. He was always a homebody until he met her."

He couldn't imagine that anyone in the Rush family could be deemed a *homebody*. Cooper and Annie's parents were both doctors and had worked in Third World countries before they set up a mobile clinic that went into the poorest communities around Florida. Coop designed software for Ajay's technology firm, which financed trips to the four corners of the world for supposed "research." And Annie used to be a sought-after photojournalist before she retired to get married and have babies.

"That's funny," he said, "because Bianca gives you the credit for inspiring her to travel the way she does."

"Me? That's ridiculous. I don't go anywhere." She leaned back against the seat.

"You used to. You led quite the life of adventure before you got married." Again, she speared him with an incredulous look, prompting him to add, "From what I've heard."

Her expression turned pensive. "That was a long time ago."

"Only ten years."

"That's a whole generation."

Reluctantly, he released her hand and checked the speed and altitude. If he maintained this course, they'd be in New York in less than three hours.

And then the real fun would begin.

"No, it's only half of a generation," he corrected her, stretching his arms behind his head. Did she really think their life experiences were so divergent? Their age difference wasn't quite that pronounced, though it certainly did exist.

He unbuckled and stood, which made her sit up in alarm.

"Want something to drink?" he asked.

"Shouldn't you concentrate on flying the plane?"

"But I always wanted to be a flight attendant," he said, feigning exasperation.

From her frown, she did not think his joke was funny.

"We're perfectly safe," he assured her. "The skies are clear and this plane has an autopilot that has logged more hours than I have. It won't take long for me to go back and grab us a couple of sodas. Caffeine-free Diet Dr Pepper, right?"

He didn't wait for her reply, certain she hadn't changed her beverage preference since the move. It was hard not to notice her cola of choice when she'd hoarded cases of the stuff. Of course, with Annie, it was hard not to notice anything.

Like the way she crinkled her nose when she was thinking. Or the way she twirled her hair around her finger when she was zoning out from exhaustion.

God, he had it bad. He was whipped, and except for that all-too-brief moment when his hand had touched hers in the cockpit, she barely knew he was alive.

Well, he was going to change all that.

He poured her drink into a glass with ice, courtesy of the plane's well-stocked galley, and then popped a plate of pre-packaged cinnamon rolls into the microwave while he brewed coffee for himself. The aroma awoke his senses, but not enough to turn him away from his purpose.

To seduce Annie Rush.

No, more than that—to win her heart.

The bet with Leo had been a lark—an added incentive and, frankly, a reason to test the concept of him and Annie hooking up on some of the people who would, by virtue of their friendships and family ties, have a say-so in whether or not the relationship worked out. As expected, Leo had not been enthusiastic about the idea. But he also hadn't dismissed it out of hand. As Cooper's best friend, he could have taken the bullying big-brother role and warned Drew away from pursuing Annie. He hadn't. He'd made a wager on his success.

Wasn't exactly a seal of approval, but it was likely the best Drew was going to get.

He returned to the cockpit.

"Wow," she said, taking a long, appreciative sniff of the warm, cinnamon-scented air. She moaned in anticipatory pleasure and Drew's brain immediately conjured images of her making those very same sounds under much more intimate circumstances.

"I aim to please," he said, reaching to the depths of his control. He slid into his seat and pulled out a tray table to hold the rolls. "You know, for someone who's seen the world, you sure do get excited by the little things."

With her hand hovering over the pastries, her fingers wiggling in anticipation of choosing precisely the right treat, she snickered. "I wouldn't call this aircraft and all its amenities a little thing. I knew your business was doing well, but I had no idea you were so stinking rich."

He checked the instruments and chuckled. "I do okay, but 'stinking rich' I am not. This plane doesn't belong to me. I have a much more humble twin-prop."

"So this belongs to?"

"Ajay Singh."

"Coop's boss?"

"Yeah, I move all his executives and I fill in as his private pilot when he's in a pinch. In return, he lets me take this baby out every so often. For special occasions."

"Like going to New York to pick up your sister's wedding dress?" she concluded.

"More like impressing *you* while we go to New York to pick up my sister's wedding dress."

"Why would you care about impressing me?"

Her question was so honest, even she seemed a little surprised by it. God, did she really have no idea?

"Natural instinct," he replied. "Men can't resist showing off their biggest, most expensive toys when a beautiful woman is around."

She nearly snorted soda up her nose. Unable to stop himself, he laughed.

"Yeah, that was really beautiful," she said, grabbing blindly for her purse as caramel-colored liquid dribbled down her shirt.

Drew reached for a towel he kept in the storage pocket beside his seat. The woman of his dreams had a sweet, syrupy drink splattered down her chin, neck and across her generous breasts. This wasn't a cleanup he could simply stand by and watch. He was, after all, a hands-on guy.

Kneeling beside her, he moved toward her with the towel, which she attempted to grab.

"What are you doing?" she asked, her voice so soft he almost didn't hear her with the steady hum of the engines in the background.

"Helping," he replied, keeping the cloth firmly in his hand.

"Drew," she said, her voice thick with warning.

He dabbed the towel on her chin first, staring hard into her eyes until her blush of embarrassment was replaced by a deeper, darker flush from her cheeks to her chest. He imagined her skin was so hot that if he didn't hurry, the soda might evaporate in one long sizzle.

"Just let me, Annie."

She closed her eyes, squeezing them tight as if she expected his touch to bring her pain instead of pleasure. Wow. Just what had that ex-husband of hers done to make her fear a man's touch—or was it only *his* touch that frightened her? Was it because of who he was and how old he wasn't—or was it because she was terrified of what he would make her feel?

Desire. Passion. Fire.

He wiped away a streak of soda slinking down her throat, licking his lips as his gaze strayed down the long, clean lines of her neck. Her flesh undulated as she swallowed hard.

"I can finish," she said, though not in a tone that demanded capitulation.

"No," he replied. "Let me."

"Drew," she said again, but his name trailed off when he leaned forward and kissed the spot on her neck he'd just wiped free.

With a sigh, she relaxed into his kiss, which emboldened him to open his mouth and taste her. The combination of saltiness and sweetness threw his senses into instant inebriation.

She placed his hands on her shoulders. "You have to stop."

"Why?" he asked, moving so he could reach the erogenous zone directly below her ear.

"Because this…is…wrong," she replied, her whisper simmering with heat he intended to stoke—if she gave him the chance.

"No, it's not," he insisted, nuzzling against her. "We're both adults and we're alone and we're attracted to one another."

"I'm not—"

She cut her own denial short when he suckled her neck harder, her earlobe tickling his nose.

"Yes, you are," he assured her. "And I'm dead tired of hiding how much I want you. Now that I've got you all to myself, I'm not letting you slip away."

3

FROM THE DEPTHS of her strength, Annie summoned the self-control to push Drew away. This time, she meant business. Allowing him to kiss her was ridiculous. Crazy. Unexpected. Shocking and…delicious.

But the madness had to stop. Before it started. Before they'd gone too far.

Drew relaxed on his haunches, his expression wholly unrepentant.

"What's wrong with you?" she asked.

He pretended to think hard. "Hmm, for starters, I don't believe the word *wrong* relates to us."

She barked out a laugh, snagged the towel from his hands and attempted to wipe the last of the cola from the front of her T-shirt, which, mercifully, was a dark shade of purple and would hide most of the stain. "There isn't a better word in the whole English language for this so-called *us*."

He dropped onto his knees so that his face was inches from her breasts. Her nipples squeezed tight, but her sturdy bra and the towel kept the evidence of her arousal hidden.

"Only when used to emphasize how *wrong* you are," he countered.

"I'm too old for you," she insisted.

His smile curved at the corners of his mouth in the most

contradictory and charming way. "All boys fantasize about older women. I'm just lucky enough to finally have a shot at you."

"You do not have a shot."

His light brown gaze dipped down her front. She gasped at the pink flush darkening her skin. After fumbling with the seat belt, she tore out of her chair.

He did not follow her, but remained in the doorway between the cockpit and the cabin, his arms braced on the threshold, making him look even more delectable with the sun kissing his long hair from behind and outlining his muscular arms.

"I could have a shot," he argued, "if you'd let go a little. Age is just a number."

She slid into one of the plush leather seats usually reserved for executives or VIPs, not single moms out for a wild weekend on behalf of their little brother's bride-to-be.

But she could be so much more. Only a few short years ago, she'd been a sought-after photojournalist dashing around the world, exploring new places, cultures and attitudes. And every so often, new men. When had all that changed so drastically?

"It's not just about our age difference," Annie said.

He ventured a few steps into the cabin. "Okay, then lay out your objections and I'll address them each individually."

She smirked. "You sound so businesslike."

"Well, I am the CEO of a successful company. I didn't get this way on my looks alone."

"This from the guy whose business is called Hunks with a Truck?"

"I didn't say looks didn't help," he confessed, his tone both mischievous and serious. "But it takes more than muscle and a dearth of shirts to make a business work."

"Trust me, the dearth of shirts doesn't hurt," she muttered, remembering just how irresistible Drew had looked last year when he was parading through her house with nothing covering his pecs but sweat and a tan.

"Well, then, that's a start."

And with that, he removed his shirt.

She wanted to object. Honest to God, she wanted to gasp in horror and order him to get dressed that very minute, young man.

Trouble was, the feelings Drew evoked in her came from the opposite direction of her motherly instincts. Or sisterly ones. Or cool aunt ones.

The most basic, intrinsic woman she'd kept hidden for so long sighed with a deep appreciation for the beauty of his impressive male form. She gulped, then leaned back in her chair, threw back her head and closed her eyes. Yes, she found him attractive. What woman wouldn't? Even her eighty-year-old grandmother would get a little thrill seeing this man shirtless.

Apparently, Drew took her posture as surrender. He slid into the seat across from hers, leaned forward so that his elbows balanced over his thighs and took her hands in his.

"Tell me you're not attracted to me," he ordered.

"I'm not attracted to you," she said automatically.

"Liar."

"True."

"Tell me you think of me as a kid."

She shook her head. She'd just proved she couldn't tell a lie that big.

"Then what's holding you back from taking what you want? How long has it been, Annie, since you've had time for yourself? How long has it been since you let a man desire you—every inch of you?"

"You've lost your mind," she concluded. There could be no other explanation. Drew could have any woman in the universe. Why on earth would he want a woman with an extra ten pounds on her hips and who smelled of sweaty baseball mitts most of the time?

"Insanity doesn't change the fact that I want to kiss you so badly, I can't see straight."

She opened her eyes, leaned forward and examined his face

carefully. She couldn't see anything but sincerity and—if his liquid irises were any indicator—true desire.

"Drew, you're so much—"

"Don't tell me how young I am," he said, and she could tell his patience was wearing thin. "I've been around for every one of my birthdays. Got presents, too. I'm twenty-six. You're thirty-eight. That's twelve years. More than a decade. And yet, I don't care."

"Maybe I wasn't going to say anything else about your age," she argued.

He challenged her with a tilted eyebrow.

"Okay, maybe I was," she confessed. "But you must have a million beautiful young girls throwing themselves at you. How could you possibly want someone who has given birth twice and has the stretch marks to prove it?"

He dropped to his knees, assuming the same posture he had in the cockpit, only here in the spacious cabin, the action seemed more gallant and romantic. Until he pressed closer and she felt the hardness and length of him against her leg.

Her eyes widened.

"If you need more convincing of what you do to me, I could always…" He seized the button at his waistband, but she stopped him by grabbing his wrists.

Another mistake. The electric surge that resulted from her hands touching his in such close proximity to his groin nearly caused her to groan out loud. She did want him, but what woman wouldn't? Didn't explain why he wanted her.

But did she really have to understand? Or could she just, for the first time in a very long while, go with the flow?

With a stranger, she might have been able to throw caution to the wind. She hadn't exactly been a virgin when she'd fallen for her ex. She'd had a few flings. She liked sex. A lot. And she missed it desperately. But this was Drew—her future sister-in-law's brother. Someone she was going to have to face every Christmas for the rest of her life.

"Drew, please don't do this," she begged.

"What? Act on the attraction we've both felt for years?"

"You know that's not true."

"Half of it is. I've wanted to be with you since before it was legal."

She leaned back in the chair and this time, the shock was longer lasting. Memories flooded back at her—of meeting Drew for the first time at Coop and Bianca's college graduation, when he'd been nothing more than a sixteen-year-old stud with incredible eyes, copious amounts of charm and a flirtatious nature she'd attributed to overactive hormones. The second time, he'd been older. A college coed, barely in his twenties. They'd been at a family picnic. Fourth of July. Her husband hadn't been with her. But Drew had spent nearly the entire day with Andy, barely two, playing trucks in the sandbox and then lighting sparklers until the child had been so hopped up and excited, Annie had barely been able to get him to sleep.

God. That meant Will had just been born. If Drew had flirted with her that weekend, she surely had not noticed, being too busy with a fussy newborn and an absentee husband.

The next time she'd crossed paths with him, however, was during spring break a few years later. She'd taken the boys to visit her parents, who were on the verge of moving into a smaller house on the water. Drew had been there when she'd arrived, working out the details of the move, which his company was handling. He'd stayed for dinner. He'd sat next to her. They'd talked nonstop, though about what, she hadn't a clue. They simply got along well. They always had.

But never once had he come on to her. Yeah, he'd flirted, but in that charming way young men did with everyone of the female persuasion. She'd never imagined that his attention meant anything more.

Until now.

She shivered, a delayed reaction to the sensation of his lips on her neck. She didn't need to feel his erection against her knee to know he wanted her—he made his intentions evident with his eyes, which were locked on hers with such intensity she couldn't look away.

His stare was hungry. Undeniable. He seemed aware of

her every breath. For the first time in forever, she felt entirely female. Not like a mom or a wife or a divorcée—like a woman.

An attractive woman.

No, more than that. Drew made her feel hot—in every sense of the word.

"Before you were legal?"

His grin was shameless. "Oh, yeah."

A soft beeping from the cockpit arrested his attention. He lifted her hands to his face, dropped a gentle kiss on her knuckles, then returned to his post. He shrugged back into his shirt as he double-checked the instruments and heading. His confession knocked the wind out of her, but in a good way—a very good way.

Her family would be scandalized—but it wouldn't be the first time she'd caused them to have apoplectic fits. From running off to be a photojournalist to marrying a laced-up corporate raider and divorcing him when she got sick of being ignored, Annie was notorious for doing things her own way. The only person this rebellious streak continued to shock was herself.

She glanced out of the circular window and couldn't imagine a more perfect day for flying. The sky was turquoise, the clouds rare and wispy and the ride smooth as glass. She'd checked the weather before they'd left Florida. This was supposed to be an easy flight.

Funny how it had turned into anything but.

He returned to the cabin. He brought the cinnamon rolls.

How could she possibly resist him?

4

DREW WATCHED ANNIE fiddle with the pastry, tearing off tiny pieces and smearing the tips of her fingers with spice and sugary icing. His mouth watered to take her sweetened skin into his mouth, but he satiated his hunger by grabbing one of the rolls and eating it whole. His ravenous action made her laugh, and her smile tipped his sugar rush into sheer nirvana.

"You're a great guy, Drew," she started.

"Ouch," he said, grabbing a second bun and suddenly wishing he had an ice-cold glass of milk to wash the deliciousness down. Not that milk would add to his image as an older-than-she-thinks guy. "At least you didn't call me nice."

She swallowed another chunk of cinnamon roll. "I happen to like nice guys."

"So your husband was a nice guy?"

She frowned, but Drew didn't need her unguarded reaction to know the truth. Her husband was an idiot. What guy landed a beautiful, exciting, intelligent woman like Annie, had two adorable kids and then ignored them for balance sheets and stock options?

Moron.

"I think it was his ambition that attracted me," she admitted. "I was shooting his picture for a magazine article on up-and-coming entrepreneurs. Confidence can be very seductive."

Drew grinned. If there was one thing he had in spades, it was the knowledge that his weaknesses were preferable to a lot of guys' strengths. He didn't deny his arrogance—he simply tried to keep it in check by remembering that karma was a bitch.

"So when did he change?"

"That's just it. He didn't change," she said. "He was the same supercharged executive from the moment we exchanged I-do's until the day he missed Will's first birthday party in order to entertain an out-of-town client. I went into the water with the corporate shark, but I just never expected to become his chum."

"You're not blaming yourself, are you?" he asked.

"Blame? I stopped assigning any of that a long time ago. It doesn't matter whose fault it is. What's done is done. We both went into the relationship with unrealistic expectations."

"Like?"

"Oh, I don't know," she sang, her lashes tipping upward as if the answer to his question was somewhere on the ceiling. "He expected me to give up everything I ever cared about in order to clean his house and raise his children, and I expected him to cancel his trip to Chicago when I had pneumonia and two children under the age of six with the flu."

She chuckled humorlessly, but Drew appreciated how hard it would be to laugh about such neglect, even if she had taken control of her life by leaving the mook behind. Just the fact that she could talk about one of the most painful experiences in her life gave him hope. Maybe she was also ready to put those memories behind her. Start over.

Hopefully, with him.

He retrieved his coffee, refreshed her drink and helped her polish off the pastries. He checked the instruments again; they were on course and making good time. The nearest tower reported very little traffic in his field of flight, but he knew he should return to the cockpit. He lured her to follow by asking a question that couldn't be answered from a distance.

"So," he started, strapping himself back into the pilot's chair, "if you and I had a relationship, what would the expectations be?"

"That's easy," she replied. "You and I would never have a relationship."

"Well, I suppose I could settle for a brief affair," he said, lying through his teeth.

She shook her head, but her eyes were alight with what he hoped were sparkles of possibility. He let his hand drift over to her lap, entwining his fingers in hers.

He leaned sideways and drew her knuckles across his cheek, inhaling the mingled scents of cinnamon and the exotic perfume she must have dabbed on her wrist.

"You sure know how to tempt a woman," she confessed.

"If that were true, you'd be kissing me on the mouth right now," he said, finally giving in to his instincts and nibbling on the tips of her fingers.

When he licked at the sugar coating her skin, she gasped, but did not pull away. He took her inaction as invitation and took one fingertip into his mouth, suckling softly until the cinnamon frosting was gone and his passion for Annie had ratcheted up to new and dangerous levels. He kissed each finger clean and moved up to her wrist. The translucent skin pulsed with her rapid heartbeat. The scent of oriental flowers and spices teased his nostrils. He looked up at her face, her eyes closed in sweet surrender, when an alarm demanded his attention.

He dropped her hand instantly and though he heard her yelp in surprise behind him, he concentrated on flying. He flipped on his headphones and spent a split second clearing his head. The warning required he check in with the nearest tower, which he did as quickly and efficiently as his addled brain could manage.

"Is everything okay?" Her voice quivered, whether from fear spawned by the alarm or from what they'd just shared, he wasn't sure.

"Yeah," he replied. "Maybe I should just concentrate on getting us to New York in one piece for a while."

"That's probably a very good idea."

"Doesn't mean I'm done with you, sweetheart."

A corner of her mouth twitched, but she effectively tamped down the smile. "That's very good to know."

OVER THE PAST EIGHT YEARS, Annie had faced many situations that made her think she'd lost her mind. When Andy had flushed his entire set of little green soldiers down the toilet. When Will had decided that her ruby red lipstick was the perfect shade for a racing stripe down the center of her great-grandmother's antique lace tablecloth. When her ex had reacted to her request for a divorce by asking if she'd picked up his dry cleaning. She'd managed to hold herself together through every crisis, though she wasn't entirely sure how.

But today, crazy didn't feel so terrifying. In fact, crazy felt downright invigorating.

As she and Drew landed in New York, unloaded their sparse belongings and headed to the hotel in a limousine he'd engaged for the occasion, she seriously considered seducing the man in the backseat.

She'd always wanted to do it in the back of a stretch. A woman who had been without a husband for a large part of her marriage and then divorced for a year couldn't exist without entertaining a few fantasies. Of course, she'd never imagined Drew Brighton as her costar in her imagined erotic interludes. But now that he'd nibbled so deliciously on her neck and fingers, told her she was beautiful and that he'd been fantasizing about her since he was a teenager, she could not think of anyone else for the role.

Despite his aversion to wearing the label, Drew was a nice guy. He was young, yes, but that wasn't his fault. If her advanced age didn't bother him, why should she get hung up on a number? He wasn't a teenager anymore. He was all man. And he was smart, breathtakingly good-looking and intense in his pursuit of her. Would the world really stop revolving or implode in a rush of fiery destruction if she let him catch her?

Just for two days?

An affair with him could not last longer than that. She was a single mother with two children. He was a young man with a booming business and a life that probably wouldn't include a wife and kids for a very long time—if ever. The only thing stopping her from jumping his bones at the first opportunity was knowing that once her brother married his sister, there would be no avoiding him after their affair ended—no pretending they hadn't had passionate sex for a wild weekend before the wedding.

Could she live with those consequences?

When he placed his hand possessively on the small of her back while leading her to the elevator in their hotel, she thought, yeah.

Yeah, she could.

As soon as the brass doors closed behind them, Annie's breath caught. The interior of the lift was entirely mirrored. How hot would it be to do it in a confined space with reflections of their bodies assailing her from every direction?

"What are you thinking?" he asked, his tone low and ripe with expectation.

Her mouth was suddenly dry. Thirsty. Parched for a drink of Drew, who was such a tall glass of ice-cold water, she thought she'd suddenly been transported to a desert on the hottest day of the year.

"Annie?"

Her gaze darted to the many mirrored surfaces all around them, and then to the security camera in the upper right-hand corner.

"Annie."

This time, her name was an admonition.

"What?" she asked, with feigned innocence.

He didn't buy her act for a minute. Dropping their bags, he grabbed her hands and pulled her flush against him, not hesitating before he covered her mouth with his.

Forceful and skilled, his kiss destroyed the last of her reluctance. His tongue did not tangle with hers, but teased and pleasured and tasted until her balance wavered. Her fingers still captured in his, he braced his hands on the small of her back, forcing her back to arch. The minute his mouth descended onto her neck, her nipples tightened and shards of need cut deep within her. When his lips touched the hollow at her throat, she moaned, a needful, mewling sound that was punctuated by the ding of the elevator announcing that they'd arrived at their floor.

Breathing heavily, Drew pulled away. He released one of her hands so he could grab their bags, but he held tight to her with the other. In silence, they found his room. Annie swiped the key card, knowing that the minute the door was closed behind them, her entire life would change.

5

DREW'S SENSES barely catalogued the scene around them. A faint orange glow of sunshine on the other side of drawn curtains. The smell of lilac and vanilla and recycled air. But the minute his lips touched Annie's, nothing else registered beyond the wildness of her mouth on his, the soft swell of her breasts against his chest, the spiced fragrance of her hair and skin and the long-anticipated feel of her flesh yielding to his. Hungry for so long, he sought to gorge himself on her until he burst with satisfaction.

"Drew, wait," she gasped.

With monumental effort, he pulled away.

"Why?"

"Is this how it should be?"

He had no idea what she was talking about. He'd take her any way he could get her.

"I don't care how I have you, but if I don't have you soon, I'm going to explode."

She placed both her hands on his chest, holding him at bay while she panted until she could breathe and talk at the same time. He knew exactly how she felt. Though he could take in oxygen just fine, his lungs were burning for another inhalation of her.

"So we came all the way to New York to rip each other's clothes off at the first opportunity?" she asked.

Her frankness knocked his brain back into sync. He'd fully intended to seduce Annie once they made it to Manhattan, but he'd planned to show a little more finesse. He swallowed thickly and pulled away, his lips buzzing from the absence of her warmth.

"I've got to be honest here," he admitted. "That scenario isn't entirely unappealing."

Her chest heaved, torturing him. So round and perfect, he wanted those breasts in his hands, in his mouth. Her eyes, dark a moment ago with desire, expanded so that the emerald color shocked him with its intensity.

"You're honestly that attracted to me?" she asked.

She still had doubts? He tried to put himself in her place, understand the situation from her point of view, but his heart was pounding in his ears and remaining vertical when all his blood was rushing downward wasn't easy.

"However much you imagine I want you, multiply that times ten. That's how many years I've lusted after you. I can't imagine not being inside you as soon as possible."

When he moved toward her, she did not flinch. In fact, her mouth opened and her tongue slipped out and moistened her lips, as if readying her flesh for his attention. But he did not kiss her. Instead, he locked his libido into pause and smoothed his hands down her sides, inhaling as the hourglass of her figure heightened his need to feverish pitch.

"And you want me, too," he argued, "or your mind wouldn't have thought such naughty things in that elevator."

She didn't deny it, though her gaze dipped momentarily to the floor. He didn't allow her reluctance to last. Crooking a finger beneath her chin, he lifted her face to his.

"Why won't you admit what you so obviously want?"

She shook her head. "I'm not used to indulging my own needs anymore."

"You're a very giving woman," he assessed, allowing his hands to roam possessively around her waist, down her back, then curving over her ass. "You put everyone else's needs above your own. But that's not what I'm asking you to do here, Annie. I want you to take what *you* want. And I hope to hell that's me."

He leaned forward and kissed her neck. After a few seconds of his attention to the taut tendons, she relaxed and arched into him. He took total advantage, blazing a path along her collarbone, nudging her T-shirt aside with his nose. He nipped at her flesh, all the time rubbing her hips rhythmically, and then smoothing his touch upward until his thumbs brushed over her nipples. She gasped, then cooed. When her nipples strained prominently against the material of her shirt, he kneaded his hands into her hair and then outlined her slightly opened mouth.

"Drew," she whispered.

"Yeah," he replied, grinning. "Feels good, doesn't it? You're so beautiful, Annie."

"What if—"

"Shh," he insisted, moving his thumbs so that they pressed against her lips. "This isn't a worst-case scenario. Don't worry about tomorrow. Although, if you want tomorrow, and the next day and the next, I'm certainly willing to provide."

He brushed a soft kiss just above her eyes, then pressed just tight enough against her so that she could feel the full length and thickness of his erection against her belly. The instinct to take away time for her to object warred with his need for her to be completely and totally on board with what he hoped like hell they were about to do.

She didn't say anything, didn't reply, didn't move. She wasn't stiff or unresponsive, but frozen in place, as if afraid to take what she wanted—what she deserved.

"Do you ache for me to touch you?" he asked. "Here."

When he cupped her breast, she moved until her flesh filled his palm. She was the perfect size. The perfect weight. Was the texture as soft as he imagined? The taste as sweet?

His vision blurred. It took the full force of his self-discipline to drop his hand lower and give her a squeeze at the juncture between her thighs. "Or perhaps here."

She cried out. The sound vibrated through him. He could hardly think. Hardly breathe.

"Let me soothe that ache," Drew begged.

Yes, *begged*. He knew it and he didn't care. He wanted her and had never imagined he'd get this close so quickly. They were alone in his hotel room and he'd already kissed her, already tasted her, already learned that she was attracted to him, even if she was coming up with a thousand reasons in her practical mind for why she shouldn't give in to temptation.

He moved back just enough so she could see his face while he applied sweet pressure through her jeans.

Annie swallowed thickly, then said the word *please* with such force, he knew it had cost her. He'd make it worth the price.

He unzipped her jeans and tugged them down her hips. She stepped out of the denim and kicked the pants away, then grabbed his shirt and pulled him to her as she leaned back against the nearest wall. Inch by inch, he drew her T-shirt over her head.

Her sweet white bra cupped breasts he'd dreamed about for longer than he could remember. They were round and full and perfectly shaped to his hands. A dark tip peaked from the demi-cup. On fire with want, he braced her curved backside and lifted her just high enough so that he could take her in his mouth.

Her skin tasted like silk. She wrapped her arms tight around his shoulders and neck and lifted herself more fully into his mouth. He feasted on her, dizzy from the sensations, high on the sound of her pleasured moans. But this wasn't enough. He wanted more. He wanted it all.

With deft hands, he released the closure on the back of her lingerie. In seconds, she was bare. And beautiful. He hardly knew what to do first.

He buoyed both breasts in his hands, pleasuring one with his thumb while he laved and suckled the other. She cried

out boldly, her hair tossing from side to side as she fought
the sensations. Then, little by little, she stopped fighting and
unbuttoned his shirt. Skin to skin, she kneaded his shoulders,
kissed his neck and tangled her fingers into his hair. He gave
concentrated attention to her earlobes, breasts and lips, but he
needed more.

With his hands on her hips, he dropped to his knees. Her
panties, also white, but trimmed with a line of lace, hid too
much. He pleasured her belly button, flicking his tongue in and
out of the tiny groove while he dragged them down her legs.

Her hands were still in his hair, so she easily tugged his
attention upward.

"Drew," she gasped.

He smiled. She was uneasy. Uncertain. He understood, but
he wasn't about to let her give in to her fears. Not when he was
this close to nirvana.

"I want to taste you," he said.

She shook her head, but without any real conviction.

"Just one taste?"

She gulped for air, then pressed hard against the wall. The
tension in her body extended down her legs so that her knees
locked. He used his hands to part the sweet curls at the top of
her thighs, exposing her pink, moist flesh. His mouth watered,
and one long lick took him over the edge. She was delicious.
Sweet. Salty. But the flavors hardly mattered. It was the way
she moved beneath him that drove him mad.

He smoothed a hand down her leg, then lifted her thigh and
placed it over his shoulder. Tilting her hips, he had complete
access, which he used until she screamed his name.

"Drew, don't," she battled. "I'm about to—"

"Yes, I know," he said between suckling her outer vulva and
manipulating her clit with a stiff tongue. "Come on, sweetheart.
Take what I'm giving. Take it."

He stopped talking. He had better uses for his mouth and
he applied them in earnest until she was crying out an aria of
nonsensical sounds that played like music to his ears. Her taste
intensified as she came and he lapped her up like nectar. He

could barely drag himself away from her until she started to shake and he suspected she might collapse.

"Drew, please."

"Don't worry, sweetheart," he said, standing. "I've just started. There's more where that came from. A hell of a lot more."

6

SHE GRABBED his shirt and pulled him to her as she leaned
back against the nearest wall. Her tendons had turned to jelly,
her muscle to mush. Every inch of her skin quivered and she
feared that the engorgement of her private parts would keep her
from walking for weeks. Luckily, Drew sensed her inability to
move and lifted her into his powerful arms. He carried her to
the bed, somehow managing to rip the comforter to the ground
before laying her on the cool, crisp sheets.

Automatically, she curled onto her side, facing him, her
knees tilted in a useless attempt to cover her nudity. If he sensed
her sudden shyness, he didn't acknowledge it. Instead, he leaned
over her and kissed her on the mouth, long and thoroughly.

"You're shaking," he said, not without a lilt of cockiness.

"You're surprised?"

"I'm rather pleased with myself, honestly. What about
you?"

"I think I'm in shock," she confessed.

"Then I'll have to cover you and keep you warm until the
shock wears away. Just give me a minute."

He kissed her once more, then disappeared down the hall
to where they'd abandoned their bags. She heard him dig into
the luggage. Once beside her on the bed, he took out a box of
condoms and a sparkling tube of sensual lubricant.

And not some over-the-counter lube, either. It was a specialty brand. She knew because she'd ordered the stuff for years. A woman didn't live with a neglectful husband and not know a thing or two about sex toys.

She tugged the sheets out from under her and wondered how he knew about her personal preference.

"Pretty confident you'd need all that, were you?" she asked.

His grin renewed the throbbing between her thighs.

"I didn't think you'd mind being protected—and pleasured." He lifted the lube bottle, shaped not surprisingly with phallic contours, and gave it a shake.

She slipped her hand under her pillow and watched wickedness dance in Drew's light brown eyes. He really was incredibly delicious. And he'd given her the first male-on-female orgasm she'd had in years—as opposed to vibrator-on-female, which she'd grown weary of.

"I don't mind, but I am wondering how you came to select that particular brand of lube. I may be dazed from what you just did to me, but I don't believe in coincidences."

"I knew you were a smart woman," he said, removing his jeans.

If he'd intended for the sight of him to distract her, he'd again maneuvered expertly. The blue material of his boxers clung to him like a second skin, outlining the proof of his arousal, as well as emphasizing his lean, six-pack abs and impressive thighs. Her lungs tightened and breathing suddenly wasn't easy or automatic.

She cleared her throat and soldiered on, though, determined not to make a fool of herself.

"How'd you know what I like?" she asked.

"I moved you last year," he replied.

"You went through my personal things?"

He reached forward and slicked a lock of her hair behind her ear. "I'm not a stalker, Annie. But if you recall, you asked me to take care of packing up your office. I'm afraid the receipt caught my eye."

She blushed. Really, honest-to-God blushed. Heat rose from her chest to her neck. Her face burned for an instant, before he laughed, leaned forward and kissed the mortification away.

"Finding that receipt made my mind up for me," Drew said. "Any woman who had the guts to take care of her own needs was a woman I wanted to be with. I wish you'd bought more on that purchase so I could know all the things you like."

She laughed, determined not to let embarrassment keep her from enjoying this amazing man. "I like you," she admitted.

What was not to like? He was handsome, charming, smart and successful. He'd just brought her a rush of pleasure she hadn't had in years, without taking a single thing for himself. And now, instead of jumping her bones when he had her naked in his bed, he was having a nonchalant conversation about discovering her sexual secrets and wanting to exploit them all.

She grabbed the lubricant and popped the top. "Let's start with what we've got and I'll try to fill you in as we go."

Though she didn't think his smile could go any broader, she'd been wrong. The grin cracked his face in two—each half more devastating than the other. He slid under the sheets with her and kissed her hungrily.

She couldn't help but instantly melt into him. His body, so lean and hard, pressed against her plump softness with utter perfection. Despite the fact that he hadn't had any satisfaction against that wall, he seemed completely content with bathing her face in kisses, then her neck, then her shoulders, then her breasts. He ramped her up to boiling point again, but instead of lowering himself and moistening her with his mouth, he retrieved the lubricant, poured a measure onto his fingers, then explored.

The first sensation between her legs was cold—bitter, intense cold that brought her nerve endings to immediate attention and soothed the skin he'd already suckled to satiation. She nearly shot up off the bed, forgetting how potently this magic potion worked when applied by a man's skillful fingers rather than slathered on the end of a waterproof, rubberized vibrator.

"Oh, Drew," she moaned.

"Yeah, baby," he growled. "Open up for me. I want to see this work on you."

He crawled downward and positioned himself between her thighs. His expression of wonder injected her with a boldness she'd never thought she'd feel again. She bent her knees and spread her thighs, opening her to his full and unhampered gaze.

"You're still shaking," he said, smoothing his fingers around her skin, teasing the tip of her clit with his deft touch.

"So cold," she managed to mutter, hardly able to break apart the barrage of sensations. The chill of the lotion. The heat of his gaze. The precision of his touch.

"Then let's get the heat started," he said, pressing his index finger into her slick passage.

Her breath caught as the cold eased deeper and pleasure blanketed her body like a snowstorm. Moving his fingers in and out, he stretched her, prepared her, built the anticipation to nearly unbearable levels.

And then the heat began.

Friction ignited the lube and turned it to liquid fire. The burning was delicious. Blood rushed to her core and whatever nerve endings might have been asleep now awoke full force. She was panting, hardly able to bring in a single gasp when she heard him flip the lid of the tube again and then smear a bit of the amazing lotion over the tips of her breasts.

"Oh, my," she said.

"Yeah, that's it, sweetheart. This is perfect timing. Enjoy that while I suit up."

Despite her best efforts to concentrate solely on the sensations of her body, she turned her head and watched him tug down his boxers. His erection was thick and taut and she longed to take him into her mouth and taste every inch of him. But before she could voice her desire, he'd donned a condom and climbed above her.

"Ready for me now?" he asked, his eyebrow tilted devilishly.

"I've never been so ready," she replied.

He reached for her hands and held them above her head while he pressed against her. She was so slick, so ready, he merged with her without much resistance, though he took the path slowly, enflaming her. When he'd reached the farthest depth, he groaned.

"Good God, Annie. I can't believe— You're...perfect."

She tried to reply, but he withdrew, then thrust forward again. Just as slowly. Just as deliciously. His neck was curved back, his eyes closed, as if in reverent prayer.

"Drew?" she said.

"One more time," he begged, retreating again with infinite slowness and then pressing in millimeter by millimeter.

She lifted her knees, tilted her hips and this time, he went deeper.

He cried out—and so did she. Not in orgasm. She, at least, was too early in the process. But she recognized the sound of his pleasured surprise—as if he hadn't truly appreciated how perfectly they would fit. She couldn't believe it, either. She'd never have imagined.

He released one of her hands, leaned forward and kissed her—but didn't move. Didn't pump into her. He denied her the friction her body so desperately wanted, even though she knew he had to be on fire, even without the lubricant igniting his skin.

"Drew?"

"Shh," he said. "I just want to savor this a second. You've got me so keyed up, it could be over in a heartbeat."

She could not resist shifting her hips a bit. He moaned rapturously. She moved again, loving how he registered every minor adjustment. He placed a hand on her hip, at first to still her, and then to help her find just the right angle, just the right direction.

"Annie, oh, Annie," he breathed.

She'd never felt so powerful. So worshipped. He spoke her name as if he'd never felt such ecstasy before. After watching the pleasure build up within him to near bursting, Annie started to lose focus. He kissed her, touched her and pumped inside her until her mind filled with colors unlike any she'd ever seen.

And then he came. He cried out with his orgasm, but did not stop moving within her except for a fraction of a second when he slipped his hand between them, touched her clit and sent her soaring.

When he finally lowered himself onto her, she accepted his warmth wordlessly. At some point, she supposed, the shock of what they'd just done would sink in.

But she hoped it wasn't anytime soon.

7

WHILE ANNIE slipped into the shower, Drew lay back against the pillows and replayed the morning in his mind. He could still taste her sweet flavors on his tongue. His nerve endings reverberated from the residual friction of her skin against his. Making love with Annie had been everything he'd imagined and anticipated—and more. If they didn't have an appointment with the designer for Bianca's wedding dress in just over an hour, he would have joined her in the bathroom and kept her in the water and steam with him until they looked like prunes.

From the moment he'd met her, he'd been fascinated by her bold love of life. Even amidst her divorce and single mother-hood, Annie hadn't backed down from challenges. She'd risen above heartbreak, but he feared she'd lost a little of herself in the process—mainly, her ability to trust.

Convincing her to have sex with him was one thing—persuading her to build a relationship was something else entirely.

And yet, he'd settle for nothing less. Sex wasn't enough to satisfy his attraction for her. Unlike many men his age, Drew always knew exactly what he wanted out of life. He didn't wander. He didn't dabble. Once Drew decided what he wanted, he went after it.

And from the moment he'd met her, he'd wanted Annie.

At first, even he'd thought his attraction to her had been nothing but a schoolboy crush. He'd run into her at events where their families mixed and he would fantasize about being old enough to win her away from her husband. But after a while, he'd realized he felt much more than infatuation. Now she was single and available. And he was old enough to turn her head.

There was the complication of her being a mom, but he'd always thought her boys were awesome. Dirty, grubby, curious and too smart for their own good, but awesome nonetheless. He hadn't thought much about fatherhood, but on the whole, the idea agreed with him.

When Leo had told them about the surprise wedding, Drew knew his chance at Annie had finally come. She'd settled into her new life. From Bianca's reports, she'd healed nicely from her husband's neglect. What issues she hadn't resolved, he'd help her with. Drew wanted Annie for the long haul—forever, if he could manage it. And this weekend was his ticket in.

Still, he was keenly aware that she had already believed in forever once and had the whole fairy tale ripped out from under her. He was going to have to convince her that risking her heart with him was no risk at all.

When she emerged from the shower in a hotel bathrobe, her skin freshly scrubbed and pink and her expression a little shy, he thought he might lose his mind with wanting her again. But he couldn't give in again so soon. He had to play this smart.

"I called the design house," he told her. "They're expecting us in about an hour."

"How does Bianca know this designer again?"

Drew grinned. With her extensive travels and bubbly personality, his sister knew someone in just about every profession from every corner of the world.

"They met when Bianca and Coop were in Belize, I think. Leo called her when he came up with the surprise wedding idea. Come to find out she had a dress in her spring collection that she thought would work perfectly. Of course, since my sister is not shaped like a coat hanger, she's remaking the original. I think she's doing the bridesmaid dresses, too, right?"

Annie shrugged. "Leo told us not to worry, so I suppose she must be. But if Joslyn Jones is a friend, isn't she coming to the wedding?"

"She's flying in for the ceremony, yeah."

"Then why couldn't she have brought the dress and fitted Bianca in Tampa?"

Drew forced his face to remain passive. That scenario had been suggested by the designer—and dismissed. Drew had wanted to sweep Annie off her feet with a trip to the big city, remind her of the daring life she'd once led, so he'd made sure things went his way.

"Her studio and all her supplies are here," he said. "So it was easier if we came to her."

"Easier for whom?"

"For her. And for me."

She chuckled. "I'd love to have been a fly on the wall when you were discussing fashion."

"Hey, I've watched a few episodes of *Project Runway*."

"And that makes you an expert?"

"No, that's why you're here," he said, unable to keep from touching her any longer. He grabbed the hem of her robe and tugged her onto the bed, rolling her beneath him. She smelled like herbal shampoo and tasted like toothpaste. In seconds, her body relaxed beneath his, completely compliant to his touch.

The pain of having to tear himself away nearly blinded him. But he had to keep his eyes on the ultimate prize. With an unrestrained groan, he grabbed his shower kit from beside the bed and headed toward the bathroom.

Even with the door shut, he heard her mutter, "So the only reason I'm here is to be a live mannequin and lend my outdated fashion sense to Bianca's beautiful wedding."

Drew laughed and cracked the door open so she could hear him loud and clear. "Honey, if that's why you think you're here, I'm not doing my job right."

SINCE DREW'S EXPERIENCE with a fashion designer's workshop was limited to the ones he'd seen on television, he was utterly surprised that Joslyn Jones's studio was a wide-open, elegant space with little fuss and no mess. The appointment-only boutique had beveled mirrors that captured the light streaming in from the glass storefront. Simple, single-garment displays showed off Joslyn's unique perspective. Wispy materials. Feminine lines. A predilection for cool blues, vibrant greens or soft grays. He wondered if the designer had a pilot's license because he'd only seen this particular palette while flying over the islands on a slightly stormy day.

"Wow," Annie said, smoothing her hands nervously up and down her jeans. "This is a showplace."

"You'll fit right in, then," he said.

She eyed him as if he'd lost his mind. "I'm pretty sure there's a peanut butter stain on the ass of these jeans."

He leaned back and perused her backside, but instantly forgot what he was supposed to be looking for. Those curves could strike a man dumb. His palms itched to tug her close, but he knew this wasn't exactly the time or the place, particularly when a young woman dressed entirely in blue-gray except for a burnished silver necklace strode into the room and welcomed them to Joslyn's salon.

"Drew? Annie?" she greeted with a smile. "I'm Tara Kennedy, Joslyn's assistant. She's just finishing up with a project and will be out in a moment. Can I offer you some wine? Bottled water?"

Annie shook her head, so Drew declined the refreshments.

After a moment of uncomfortable silence, Annie stepped toward the nearest display—an asymmetrical blouse in various shades of green paired with a slim skirt in stark white. "These clothes are lovely," she said, though she kept her hands tucked deep in her pockets, as if afraid she might get something on the designer duds if she dared touch them.

Tara beamed. "These are from Joslyn's spring collection. Would you like to try something on while you wait?"

Annie took a step away from the clothes. "Oh, no. I mean, I'm only here to have Joslyn fit Bianca's gown. I probably can't afford anything in here."

Tara laughed lightly and gave a furtive glance toward Drew, which Annie, in her embarrassment, didn't seem to notice. "Joslyn loves Bianca and wants this whole experience to be special for you, as well. Maybe after you've tried on the gown, you'll be more in the mood. Would you like a seat or maybe a tour of the workroom?"

Annie's nervousness visibly multiplied. Though he couldn't understand why, she clearly didn't think she belonged in a high-end clothing store. Hell, he didn't know anyone who deserved pretty things more than Annie.

"I'd love to see where the real work is done," he said.

"Most people do," Tara answered. "Joslyn rarely lets customers back into the inner sanctum, but for your sister, she's pulling out all the stops."

The workroom was as light and airy as the boutique up front, but decidedly more active. The whirr of sewing machines and fizz of steamers filled the air, as well as music that reminded Drew of his last trip to Jamaica. Kettledrums and flutes and the pluck of a metal-stringed guitar set the tempo. A half-dozen people scurried from workstation to workstation, handling fabric or drawings while another six or so remained stationary and concentrated on finishing seams, hand-painting material or stitching zippers and buttons onto blouses, skirts, pants and a very sparkly evening gown.

The colors in this room were definitely more varied than out front. In fact, Drew was feeling as if he'd stepped into a revolving rainbow when a tall, elegant black woman stepped forward, her hand extended and her smile dazzling against her rich cocoa skin. Like Tara, she was dressed in blue-gray. Must be the hottest color of the season—or else, the uniform.

"You're Bianca's brother, all right. You have the same eyes." She moved with the grace of a dancer and was nearly as tall as Drew. She held out her hand and gave him a surprisingly firm shake. Despite such close proximity, she narrowed her gaze and leaned forward to look into his eyes even more closely. "No, your shade is more champagne. Hers are honey-amber. That's how we met, your sister and I. I stopped her in a bar to ask if I could look into her eyes."

Drew didn't quite know how to respond to that. Luckily, Annie spoke up.

"Did you use the color in your next collection?"

Joslyn's laugh was deep, throaty and sexy. She bent and gave Annie a warm hug, as if they'd known each other for a long time. "The critics went berserk. I made a mint. If I gaze into Drew's eyes quite a bit while you're here, you won't be jealous, will you?"

Annie tried, not entirely successfully, to hide the pink that blossomed on her cheeks. "His eyes are intoxicating. A woman could lose herself in them, if she isn't careful."

He slipped his hand onto the small of Annie's back. "They're just brown eyes," he said.

Joslyn circled him and gave him a complete once-over. "The rest of you isn't bad, either. Ever do any modeling? I'm thinking of expanding into a menswear line."

Drew rubbed his hand over his nose, mouth and chin, trying not to laugh. "Not unless you count the homemade superhero costumes my sister used to dress me up in when I was six."

The humor broke the tension. Joslyn chuckled and Annie scooted away to ooh and aah over Joslyn's work, which jump-started the designer into giving them a full tour. After about fifteen minutes, however, Tara appeared with a garment bag draped gingerly over her arm.

"Are we ready for the fitting?"

Annie's smile faded.

"The models I work with usually strip down out in the open, but I'm assuming you'd like a little privacy?" Joslyn asked.

Annie nodded.

Tara gestured toward the showroom out front. "We have a dressing room in the boutique. I'll show you the way."

"Drew?" Annie asked after she'd taken a few steps, but he had not followed.

"I'll be out in a minute," he reassured her, exchanging the briefest, conspiratorial glance with Joslyn, who responded with a barely perceptible nod.

Annie narrowed her eyes, but had no option but to leave after Tara backed up and took her gently by the hand. Once she was out of earshot, Drew turned back to Bianca's friend.

"Okay, so what do you really have for me?"

Joslyn's expertly arched brow tilted upward. "You didn't give me much to go on when you called to verify our appointment. You just said you wanted something special for Annie."

"Trust me," he said, lowering his voice even though there was no way Annie could overhear, "whatever makes her feel beautiful will work in my favor."

8

"IT'S THE UNDERWEAR," Tara assessed, her French-tipped nails lightly tapping her cheek as she considered Annie's silhouette from several different angles.

Annie frowned into the full-length mirror, giving a silent nod that the dress didn't look half as stunning on her as when Tara had unveiled it on a hanger. A whispery confection of pale eggshell silk with threads of iridescent blue-green embroidery, the dress had sapped Annie's breath. Simple, yet elegant, with natural lines that evoked a singular, breathtaking wave hitting the beach at sunrise, the dress fit Bianca's personality to perfection. How it would fit her body was another matter altogether.

"Definitely the underwear," Joslyn agreed.

"I'm not wearing any underwear," Annie confessed, keenly aware that Drew had not yet emerged from the workroom.

"Well, then, there you have it," Joslyn declared with a loud clap of her hands. "We don't call good lingerie *foundations* for nothing. Most bodies require a little extra help to make a garment fit just right."

Annie turned back to the mirror. "Bianca's probably thinner than I am."

Joslyn waved her hand dismissively. "No, she isn't. That girl has a very healthy appetite and muscles from all the hiking and surfing she does. Besides, the dress looks phenomenal as it is, but it will look spectacular with a little boost in the right places. Let me make a few adjustments to the hem and side seam while Tara gets what we need."

Two other assistants emerged from the work area, but still Drew did not return. Annie felt silly asking after him—he'd done his job in delivering her to the salon. He'd probably sneaked out a back door to find a ballgame at the nearest sports bar. Besides, did she really want him to see her like this? Looking less than perfect in a dress that likely cost ten times as much as her mortgage payment?

She considered the fact that maybe he should see her. Maybe then he'd realize that she wasn't young and pert and slim like most women his age.

Of course, he'd already seen her naked. From several different angles. If that wasn't going to discourage him, this lovely dress certainly wasn't.

Joslyn and her team tucked, pinned, measured and cut for a good twenty minutes before they were satisfied. Then Tara reappeared with a beautiful box. The double *J*'s of Joslyn's logo gleamed on top and inside, wrapped in pale blue-and-green tissue, lay the most beautiful corset and matching panties that Annie had ever seen. She held it out in front of her, then blushed profusely when one of the male assistants looked up and grinned.

At the sight of her obvious mortification, he laughed. "Honey, this is the New York fashion scene. No one around here is uptight or shy."

"No one except me," she answered.

"I thought you were a famous photojournalist," Joslyn murmured, pins still stuck in her mouth. Even in her elegant cashmere blouse and slacks, she'd dropped to the floor to double-check the hem. "Bianca told me all about you."

"Bianca told you all about my past. Nowadays, I'm just a single mom with two kids."

Joslyn moved the last of the pins out of her mouth and into

the palm of her hand. "You're not *just* anything, Annie. Not while you're in my shop."

Annie smiled shyly, then agreed to put on the lingerie while the assistants took the dress to the back room to make the changes. Before she disappeared behind the curtain of the dressing room, Tara volunteered to bring out the dress Joslyn had selected for Bianca for the rehearsal.

"It laces up in the back, so it should fit Bianca fine."

Annie forced a smile. She'd expected this afternoon to be a little more fun. Trying on designer clothes in expensive surroundings, experiencing a world so removed from her own that she might as well have flown to another planet, had promised a break from the monotony of her life. But instead, she was coping with body issues and uncharacteristic shyness. She'd been bold with Drew earlier, but not nearly as confident and brazen as she'd been when she was younger. Where had that formidable woman gone?

The lost vixen returned a bit once Annie slipped into the glorious lingerie. The corset top cinched her breasts, lifting them to pre-nursing heights. Her stomach flattened and her derriere curved higher. She'd always thought underwear had to be black or red to be sexy, but this sweet nothing, in the same pale eggshell of Bianca's gown, set off Annie's skin and made her eyes pop even greener. Still wearing the strappy gold sandals her sister-in-law would wear for the wedding, she looked like a million bucks.

And where was Drew?

Tara returned, sliding a beautiful, butter-yellow dress into the room. She gave Annie time to slip it over her head, then came in and tied the criss-cross stays in the back. When Annie turned toward the mirror, Tara's smile was startling.

"Now, that, my dear, is how one wears that dress."

Annie couldn't believe her eyes. She suddenly had curves in all the right places and the color, while more suited for Bianca than her, picked up the honey highlights in her red hair.

"Bianca's going to look beautiful," she said on an amazed breath.

"You look beautiful."

Only it wasn't Tara who had made this assessment—it was Drew.

Joslyn's assistant stepped out of the way so that Annie could emerge from the dressing room. Drew sat in one of the plush chairs in the center of the boutique and she couldn't help but add a little sashay to her walk as she strode in front of him, directly across from the huge mirror. Before she turned and faced her reflection, she noted how his light brown gaze was now dark and intense. She'd seen arousal in his eyes only a few hours ago, but it was nothing compared to now. If the room wasn't filled with windows and strangers, he might have ripped that dress off her right on the spot.

The feeling was intensely powerful.

"Won't your sister look lovely?" she asked, twirling so that the soft material fluttered around her legs, revealing a slit she hadn't realized was there.

Drew swallowed hard enough for her to see his Adam's apple bob. "I'm not thinking about my sister."

Tara laughed, probably to break the sensual tension spiking through the room. Somewhere in the back of her consciousness, Annie heard the woman explain how the bridesmaid's dresses were similar in style, but were a lovely, light sage-green that would complement the emerald in Annie's eyes.

Drew leaned forward, his elbows on his knees, then glanced at the rack of clothes Tara had rolled out from the workroom into the salon.

"What else does my sister get to wear once she's wed?"

Tara darted to the collection and pulled out a sweet little sundress, an elegant pantsuit and two incredibly revealing swimsuits. She chattered while she moved them into the dressing area for Annie to try on, but before Annie could follow, Drew grabbed her wrist.

"Don't take off the underwear," he warned quietly.

Heat suffused through her body. "You're not getting all hot over your sister's sexy underthings, are you?"

"Hers is boxed up in the back, ready for our trip home. I bought this one for you."

She stepped back in surprise. Drew stood, still holding tight to her wrist. His grin was pure sin, which melted her insides to a goo not unlike her favorite lubricant—cool at first, but insanely hot once he applied some friction.

"This is mine?" she asked.

"And an outfit for tonight."

"Tonight?"

He said nothing more, but left her shivering with anticipation. The man certainly was full of surprises, not the least of which was that for the first time, he didn't look at all like the young man she'd made up her mind that he was. Drew was an old soul—one that must have seduced countless women in a hundred lifetimes and now knew exactly what he was doing.

The rest of the afternoon passed in a haze. Annie dutifully tried on Bianca's clothes, discarding her magical merry widow only to try Bianca's bathing suits, both of which succeeded in striking Drew dumb. And she'd accomplished that without any help from enchanted underwear. In fact, in the single-shouldered, cutout one-piece, she accepted that her body really wasn't so bad.

She did a lot of running around. A lot of lifting. She even jogged a few miles every other morning when her father came by to make the boys breakfast, a daily ritual that helped fill the gap of male influence in their lives. In the right clothes, she looked hot.

And with the right man watching her, she felt like the inside of a crucible.

An hour later, she was about to step back into her ordinary clothes when Tara knocked on the threshold beside the door.

"Aren't we done?" Annie asked, surprised when Tara slid in another zippered bag.

"Bianca's clothes are boxed up and the dress will be ready before you guys take off for Florida. This is for you."

She leaned out of the curtain, expecting to see Drew, but he'd abandoned his chair.

"From Drew?"

Tara grinned. "These are from a retail line Joslyn is considering for Nordstrom. Designer, but with an everyday, everywoman feel."

Inside the garment bag, Annie found a pretty, pale green bra, matching panties, a flouncy, short white skirt and an ocean-hued silk-blend top with three-quarter length fluttery sleeves and a plunging neckline. Two boxes—one with the gold shoes for the wedding and another with pale green high-heeled sandals that matched the blouse—arrived next. She immediately donned the outfit, hissing with pleasure at the final look.

"I sure hope Joslyn decides to do that line, because I'll buy out Nordstrom's with my retirement fund if I have to," she said, giving her ass one more impressed look.

Tara gave a little bow. "I will pass along your compliments."

"And my thanks, please."

Tara opened her arms for a warm hug, utterly unexpected from such a fashionable New Yorker. "You're more than welcome. Joslyn is trapped on a business call, but promises to see you at the wedding."

Annie gathered her belongings, her old clothes tucked away in a designer Joslyn Jones shopping bag. She felt incredibly rich and elegant walking out of the shop, stopping dead when she spied Drew leaning against the hood of a bulky Hummer limousine.

He wolf whistled.

She smiled, then sauntered closer to him. With each step she took away from the boutique, she felt her old self bursting through—the sassy woman she'd been when she was jetting around the world, taking pictures that were published in *National Geographic* and *The New Yorker*. Not that she was ever a fashion maven. She existed in vintage jeans and hand-me-up T-shirts from Coop. But now that she was older and wiser, she needed to be smarter about how she looked. Not for Drew. Not for any man. For herself.

"What's the car for?" she asked silkily, leaning on one hip to give him the full effect of her shapely legs.

He bit his lip hard and shoved his hands deep into his pockets, as if it took every ounce of his power to keep them to himself.

"I hired it to take us around town."

She handed her packages to the driver, then climbed inside. The interior was a gloriously decadent combination of black leather and neon lights. The ceiling glittered with tiny lights and the seats curved in undulating patterns that made no question of this vehicle's wicked decadence. In another time or place, Annie might have found the car tacky—but here and now, she was incredibly turned on.

Though she had not divulged her secret fantasy about making love in a luxury limo, she suspected—hoped—he'd guessed. Either way, she was determined to get another fantasy fulfilled. Wasn't that, after all, what this trip was about?

9

THE MOMENT the car pulled away from the curb, Drew gasped. Annie had climbed atop his lap and was unbuckling the top of his jeans.

"Where are we going?" she asked, her voice a hot whisper in his ear.

He had to think. She'd started assaulting his neck with long, languorous licks and the only destination in his mind was heaven.

"To...a...spa."

She tugged his shirt out of jeans, then ripped the tee over his head. "Tell the driver to take his time."

Drew retained clarity long enough to inform the driver that they didn't want to arrive at their destination for at least a half hour, though he amended his order to forty-five minutes when Annie slipped out of the flouncy blouse and shimmied out of the skirt. Without saying another word, she removed his pants and boxers, tossing them aside, and then directed him with forceful but wordless motions to spread his legs wide.

Her intentions were utterly illicit, painfully naughty and irresistibly awesome. He didn't dare move, especially after she dropped to her knees and took his dick in her hands.

"This is one fine instrument you've got here, mister."

He swallowed, hoping he had enough moisture in his mouth to manage a few words.

"It's finer when it's played," he replied.

She ringed her fingers at the base of his erection and tugged upward. "I'm no virtuoso."

As she stroked him until blood thrummed in his ears in time with the heavy bass of the song playing over the limo's speakers, he muttered, "You're playing my song just fine."

"I don't know," she said wickedly. "I think this song needs vocals."

When she wrapped her lips around him, Drew nearly lost his mind. He instantly tangled his hands into her hair, loving the feel of the soft silk strands against his palms almost as much as he cherished the intimacy of her mouth on his sex. She sucked him, licked him and toyed with his tip with her tongue and teeth. He was certain he was going to lose it when she tightened her grip on him and kept his release at bay.

"What are you doing?" he asked, breathless.

She ran her tongue over her lips, pleased with herself. She obviously got off on the power of it, which heightened his arousal to levels he'd never felt before. His sweet Annie had a naughty streak he'd never anticipated—not to this degree. What exactly had he gotten himself into?

"I'm learning what you like," she replied. "You're so big and thick. I'm getting wet just imagining having you inside me again. I'm going to be on top this time. And I'm going to ride you until we both come."

And she did. With more clarity of thought than he figured she could muster, she removed a condom from a box beside the backseat—a box he had not noticed before. She found a strawberry-flavored one, then tugged it over his engorged length and sucked him even more. From the way she let his head ripple over the ridges inside her mouth to the intensity with which she grasped him, she toyed with him until the brink of orgasm was only seconds away. Then she stopped, tore her thong to the side and mounted him.

She was wet and hot and insatiable. He moved aside the

cups of her dainty bra and sucked her nipples with no mercy; she cried out with pleasure and increased the tempo of their mating until they were a blur of movement. His orgasm came without warning, but she joined him seconds later, pumping until she'd taken her fill.

"Wow," he managed, though he wasn't sure if the ability to speak in complete sentences was going to return anytime soon.

She leaned her forehead on his shoulder, panting, then raked her hair out of her face and stared at him unabashedly. "Didn't wear you out, did I?"

"You kidding? As you keep pointing out, I'm a young man. Takes more than one horny cowgirl to put me down for the count."

She tilted her eyebrow and nibbled at her lips with blatant expectation.

"You ready to put your money where your mouth is?"

He flicked the strap of her new lingerie. "Already have, but if you want more, I'm game."

"Good," she said, leaning forward to kiss him thoroughly. "Because I'm playing to win."

FOR THE REST OF THE AFTERNOON, Drew attempted to regain the upper hand in his seduction of Annie Rush, but he never quite managed to top what she'd initiated in the back of the Hummer. After forty-five minutes of incredible sex, they headed to a salon where she had layers added to her short red hair and he had his mop trimmed before they shared a manicure, pedicure and facial. They ended the indulgence with a couple's massage in a room scented by eucalyptus and then soaked in a hot tub that pushed their self-control to the limit since making love in the spa was strictly forbidden. After a quick trip back to the hotel for a shared bath, they'd dressed, grabbed a few slices of New York–style pizza and then headed to an art gallery in Soho that was showing the work of one of Annie's former colleagues.

Annie jabbered constantly throughout the exhibit, telling

him about the artist's techniques, lighting and styles and waxing poetic about the locations of the shots, which she'd also visited at one time or another. By the time the gallery closed, she gripped his hand ever so slightly tighter than she had when they'd gone inside.

They made love quietly that night and held each other as they slept. The next morning, Drew coaxed Annie out of the bed with a promise of another amazing day in the city, but which she countered with a quickie in the shower before they left. They spent the day as tourists, popping into museums and shops, riding the ferry around to see the Statue of Liberty, hanging out in Times Square to lose themselves in the anonymity of the crowd.

That night, they savored a long meal at a tiny French bistro that had been recommended by several locals. The rich meal and abundant wine inspired them to stroll back to the hotel, enjoying the neighborhood while they talked about his life, her loves and the craziness that was Little League.

"I can't believe you did all this," she said, hooking her arm into his and leaning softly against his shoulder.

He inhaled her sweet, scented hair, then placed a soft kiss on the crown of her head. "I'm glad you enjoyed yourself."

She laughed. "Enjoyed myself? Drew, you tapped directly into my every fantasy."

He slipped his arm out of hers and put it around her waist, pulling her flush against him. They were under a streetlamp. The sidewalk wasn't crowded, but it wasn't deserted, either. He felt a few people shift to get around them, but he didn't care. He had to tell her how he felt at this perfect, glorious moment. "Annie, I'd move heaven and earth for you."

Her smile reached deep into her emerald irises, but he still spied a sense of disbelief amid her outward happiness. Maybe it was the way she tilted her head. Or the slight quiver in her chin.

"You've moved me in more ways than you think," she said.

"But is it enough to last beyond our flight home tomorrow?"

Her smile instantly turned bittersweet.

He had his answer.

When they reached the corner of a busy intersection, Drew hailed a cab. They slid into the backseat and held hands like teenagers all the way back to the hotel, not uttering a single word. By the time they reached their destination, Drew had difficulty figuring out how much to tip the driver with his mind reeling at all they'd shared—and all they hadn't.

To keep the wedding on schedule, they had to leave New York in the morning. He only had a few more hours to convince Annie that they should be together. Publicly. And hopefully, permanently.

"Let me get some of those," she said, indicating the packages they'd collected during their long day.

"I'm fine. Why don't you go on upstairs? I'm going to check with the front desk and make sure they cancelled your room."

With a hint of reluctance, she did as he asked. He needed a few minutes to think—tonight was his last shot. After verifying that the hotel had credited them for the second room they'd never used, he detoured into the gift shop, hoping for a little inspiration.

And a little more time.

He gravitated toward the jewelry counter and was immediately struck with an idea. In the last two days, he'd appealed to the woman he knew that Annie used to be—adventurous, sexual, fearless. If he wanted her to see him as a part of her very real, very ordinary everyday life, he had to show her he appreciated the woman she was now.

The woman she'd always be.

He took his time choosing just the right gifts and had them individually boxed. When he reached the room, he discovered the bathroom door closed and heard water running.

He knocked lightly. "Annie?"

"Hey, Drew," she said, opening the door a crack. Her eyes were puffy, but he couldn't tell if she'd been crying or if she'd simply rubbed too hard while removing her eye makeup.

"You okay?"

"I had to call my kids."

She sniffed, blotted her face with a towel and put on her best smile.

Everything was not okay.

"What's wrong?" he asked,

"With the boys? Nothing. They're having a great time with their grandparents."

She probably missed Andy and Will like crazy. After hearing her talk about them off and on through out the day, even he missed them. The idea, however fleeting, of being their stepfather filled his chest with emotion.

He clutched the gift shop bag tighter. He had one last shot at her. After tonight, he might not get another chance.

"Why don't you finish in there and I'll order up some wine," he suggested.

"Didn't we polish off two bottles at the restaurant?"

"Brandy, then?"

"Are you trying to get me drunk?"

"Only if it'll help me get lucky again," he answered.

"You don't need booze for that and you know it," she said, her grin reappearing.

"Then we'll just sip to celebrate the end of a spectacular day."

Room service brought up a bottle of his favorite Armagnac, two snifters and a small silver platter of crystallized pear, a nice accompaniment Drew never would have thought of. He stripped down to his boxers and set the tray on the bed, dimming the lights and fiddling with the clock radio on the nightstand until he found a station with mellow music. Love songs from any number of eras, from hers to his and beyond. When she finally emerged from the bathroom, she was wearing the beautiful cream-colored corset and panties.

She took a minute to strike a sexy pose with the golden light from the bathroom behind her, outlining her silhouette in ways that made Drew hard all over, and then she slowly stretched across the bed, belly down. The sight of her curvaceous bottom forced him to grab a snifter and inhale deeply before he totally forgot his intentions.

She snaked her fingers around the stem of her drink and drew it close to her lips, but did not sip. "You were downstairs a long time."

He sipped the brandy. The smooth golden liquid eased down his throat, creating a warmth that intensified as he looked into her hooded eyes. "I had last-minute shopping to do."

His mouth watered as she shifted on the bed, leaning forward so that her nipples peeked a bit out of the top of the corset. She picked a cube of crystallized pear out of the tray, popped it in her mouth, then closed her eyes as the sweetness dissolved on her tongue. She finally took a sip of the liqueur, and hummed her appreciation for the combined flavors.

"You're killing me," he confessed.

Her eyes fluttered open, but she did not pretend innocence. "I need to pay you back for all you did for me on this trip. You made me feel very sexy. Very…desired."

"That was my intention."

"You definitely succeed when you put your mind to something."

He took another swallow of Armagnac. "Here's hoping."

He took out the five boxes and put them on the bed.

Her eyes widened. "More?"

"It's nothing expensive," he assured her. "Just a little something to remember me by."

She looked at him with mock exasperation. "A little something?"

"A few little somethings," he conceded. "Open this one first."

One box was long and inside was a simple silver charm bracelet. The metal sparkled against her skin and he could not resist lifting her wrist to his mouth and placing a slow, sexy kiss on her pulse point. She'd dabbed perfume there, he guessed, or else she had the most intoxicating natural scent he'd ever inhaled. He could lose himself in the heady fragrance for the rest of his life.

If she'd only give him a chance.

She broke the spell by lifting one of the tiny boxes and opening it to reveal a charm.

"This one," he said, indicating the tiny baseball mitt, "is for Andy. It's a first baseman's glove. See the length of the fingers and the way they're all stitched together? And it's a lefty."

She set her drink down and sat up, drawing one of her hands across her breasts as if to cover up at the mention of her son. Drew pried her hand away and took time to bathe each of her fingers in languid kisses.

"I never told you Andy was left-handed," Annie said, her breath catching.

"I noticed."

"When?"

Her surprise was evident, but he shrugged. "We played catch one day during the move. He's got a wicked arm. I'm surprised he's not a pitcher, but I'm glad he's not. They can burn out too fast at his age." Grabbing another box—he'd had the salesperson top each box with a different colored bow so he could tell them apart—he said, "This is for Will. It's a—"

She took the tiny charm out of the box and leaned across him to spy the jewelry in the light from the dim lamp. Her satiny lingerie scraped across his skin like a match, inflaming him so that he could hardly think. Luckily, she finished his sentence for him.

"It's a yo-yo!"

Will, though only six, was a prodigy. Drew remembered watching the kid manipulate the toy and string for hours. He'd also helped the boy pack a collection of the vintage toys that might have rivaled a museum's. He had wooden ones, plastic ones, glass ones—and now a silver one his mother could wear on her wrist to remind her of her son's extraordinary talent.

She turned and looked at him with liquid eyes. "He spends every penny of his allowance on these things. Drew, this is the sweetest thing you could have done."

"I know you love your boys, Annie. I know how important they are to you. But," he said, picking up the third box, "there are other things that are important to you, too. Or at least, they should be."

From the sudden frown on her face, he guessed she already knew what was inside the box before she opened it. He hadn't had time to come up with anything particularly insightful or unique. Sometimes, you just had to surrender to the obvious—which he hoped like hell she'd do.

Wasn't it obvious how he loved her? Worshipped her? Cared for her and her family?

"It's a camera," she said.

"You should take pictures again," he said.

"I am," she replied, hardly hesitating.

"What?"

She laughed. "See, you don't know everything about me, Drew Brighton."

"No, I suppose I don't. What made you start again?"

She shrugged, as if the decision to return to her old profession was a fluke or a hobby, when he knew that simply wasn't the case. "The boys are old enough to be in school and I needed to pay the bills. I've sold a few shots to some local magazines. I have one or two waiting for approval at a small national publication. It's not much, but technology has changed a lot and I'm developing a new style because of it."

"You'll be fantastic," he assured her.

She frowned a little doubtfully. "I only unpacked the camera about two months ago, but it felt good to have it in my hand again. I was good, you know?"

He laughed. "Yeah, I know. Here I was hoping that this little knickknack would get you back into the business."

"I can't exactly travel around the world for a photograph anymore."

"I bet the boys would love to go cool places. Schools have holidays. And you have a pilot at your beck and call. Which leads me to this…"

The fourth box was anti-climactic, but the tiny airplane made her smile nonetheless. "Is this so I won't forget our trip?" she asked.

"This is more than just a trip," Drew insisted, pushing the tray of drinks and jewelry boxes aside to draw her so close.

"It's a fantasy," she insisted, kissing along his chin. The tiny nips were like miniexplosions, each attempting to destroy his line of thinking. But he couldn't allow it. He wanted her so much, he was certain his body would implode with need. But they were leaving in less than twelve hours. Then the craziness of the wedding would sweep them both away. He had to put his cards on the table now.

"It's not a fantasy," he said softly. "I'm in love with you, Annie. I have been for as long as I can remember."

This time when she laughed, even lightly, Drew did not appreciate it. He was pouring his heart out to her. He didn't see any humor.

He pushed her away. The move was gentle, but she was still surprised.

"Drew, you can't be serious."

"Why can't I be? Because you're old?"

She rolled entirely off the bed, the charms bouncing on the mattress. "I'm not old!"

"I'm glad to hear you say that. And for the record, I'm not young."

"That's debatable," she snarled.

"Then debate me," he challenged. He'd had enough of trying to seduce her into realizing that his feelings were real. Maybe she needed to see him at his worst before she'd realize that he was the best man to partner her for the rest of her life.

"I don't want to fight," she said.

"Then don't."

"I don't know what you want from me."

She assumed a combative stance—fists on her waist, hip jutting to the left.

He smoothed his hands over his hair, then settled them behind his head against the headboard. "That's easy. I want forever."

10

ANNIE SUDDENLY BECAME KEENLY AWARE of what she was wearing, how she was standing. She must look ridiculous, constrained by sexy lingerie and arguing with a handsome, charming, thoughtful man because he wanted a future with her and she…didn't?

No, that wasn't true. What woman wouldn't want Drew? He was sexy. Considerate. Romantic. Self-supporting. And God help her, attentive. He had, after all, waited a heck of a long time to pursue her.

And yet, she couldn't wrap her mind around the idea of them being together for more than this last night in New York City. A quickie affair was one thing. But a real relationship?

Her throat was dry. She headed toward the bathroom, but Drew leaped off the bed and blocked her path.

"I want to be with you, Annie."

She attempted to dodge around him, but her foot caught the corner of the bed and she was headed for the floor until Drew scooped her up by the waist and set her on her feet. His strong arms held her still, her back against his amazing chest.

"Stop doing that!"

"Doing what? Keeping you from falling flat on your face?"

"Trying to rescue me," she insisted. "I'm not a damsel in

distress. I didn't need you to sweep me off on your white horse to the castle in the big city. I didn't need new gowns or a new hairstyle or to feel like…to feel like…"

Like a woman?

Drew released her. She spun around in time to see him cross his arms over his chest, emphasizing not only the massiveness of his pecs but the depth of his determination.

"I wasn't trying to rescue you. I was trying to seduce you."

"Well, you succeeded," she said, straightening her corset. "Happy?"

"Not nearly."

She glanced at the closet for her robe, but it was in the bathroom. Despite her lack of clothes, she had to stand her ground and convince him that they didn't stand a chance. How could they?

But why couldn't they? She was over her ex, that much was certain. But what wasn't so written-in-stone was the condition of her heart. The very things that had attracted her to her husband had been the reasons why their marriage fell apart. What if the same happened with Drew? Could she survive another heartbreak? Could her children?

She couldn't take the chance.

"I can't give you anything more," she said.

"That's a lie," he countered, though a chuckle in his voice betrayed that he found her denial ever-so-slightly amusing.

Well, she wasn't trying to be funny. She was dead serious.

"I'm not ready for another relationship."

Even she heard the lack of conviction in her voice.

"Because your husband hurt you?"

"No," she insisted. "That's old news."

She moved again to walk away, but this time, Drew stopped her with a gentle hand on her arm. "But not an old hurt. Look, your husband was a moron. You know it. You also know that I'm not a moron. I know how spectacular you are, Annie. And I would never ignore you or your children. We'll be a family.

And at night, we'll be a couple who can't keep their hands off each other. Annie, I promise, I'll take care of you."

Her throat tightened. His eyes brimmed with complete sincerity—the kind of expression she didn't think she'd ever seen before.

She could fill rolls and rolls of film with all the things she didn't know about Drew Brighton. But what she did know counted for a lot. His need for her was intense and powerful, but Drew wouldn't burn out like her ex had. Look how long he'd taken to pursue her. He was a man who simmered, stoked, flamed. And when necessary, cooled. Here she was, standing in front of him nearly naked, and his eyes held a confidence that came from deep within.

"I don't need someone to take care of me."

"I'm not talking about needs," he said, his fingers now trailing up her arm, the friction barely there, and yet, she was aware of every sparking nerve ending. "What about *wants?* You never mention those. You have the necessities. Great kids. A great family. And soon, a great career again. But is that really enough? Do you want to go through life without someone to share yourself with?"

"I'll find that," she said, forcing the words out of her mouth. "Someday."

He stepped closer. It would be so easy to lean into him, bury herself in his strength, lose herself in his…dare she think it? Love?

"Why not today?" he asked, his voice a potent whisper against the cacophony in her mind. "And don't blame my age again because it's a lame argument and you know it. There's nothing a man ten years older has that I don't. Nothing more that he can give you. I'm giving you my heart, Annie. My soul. No man can give you more."

Annie's lips quivered, but she'd be damned if she would cry over all he offered—all she felt obligated to resist.

She was stronger than him.

More determined.

More…alone.

She made it as far as the bathroom before the tears blinded her. A sob caught in her throat and when she paused to breathe, Drew gently wrapped his arms around her waist.

"I'm afraid," Annie finally said, admitting the truth that had been pounding its way up from deep in her gut. Drew frightened her. Scared her to the depths of her consciousness. What he felt for her was so honest and palpable—she'd never encountered anything as powerful as love so freely given.

"I won't hurt you," Drew promised. "I love you. I love your children. I love your family. Hell, I'm going to *be* your family by Sunday night whether you like it or not. Give me a chance. Give us a chance."

"Yes, you are going to be family," she said, heaving in a great gulp of breath so that she could speak amid her ridiculous tears. "No matter what happens between us, we'll always be in each other's lives."

He buried his nose in her hair and, though she did not think it possible, held her tighter. "I'm counting on that. And I'm counting on what happens between us being fantastic. Glorious. Worth waiting a lifetime for."

He turned her around and grabbed a towel to wipe the tears from her face. The complete love and faith in his eyes as he dabbed at her cheeks chased the last of her doubts out of her. She had no fight left—she had no reason to fight. Drew was everything she'd always wanted in a man, but had been afraid did not exist.

"I can't believe this is happening," she confessed.

He chuckled. "What's happening?"

"I'm falling in love with you, you idiot."

This time, his laugh was deep and infectious. He pulled her close and her body melded into his. Hard to soft. Straight to curved. Male to female.

"I'm the idiot? You're the one fighting the natural order of things, lady. I love you, Annie. I've loved you too long for that to ever change."

She skewered his hair with her hands. "What if I'm not who you've built me up to be?"

"Impossible," he said. "I've seen you at your best. And I've seen you at your worst, when you were trying to hold things together, moving your whole world, dealing with emotions you'll never have to feel again."

He kissed her long and hard, and with every thrust of his tongue, every caress of his fingers, she knew she had to be with him. Had to have him. Had to see if she had another shot at a forever love.

"This is crazy insane," she decided.

"You don't have enough crazy insane in your life. I want you, Annie. I don't know what else I can do or say to convince you."

She couldn't think of a single thing. He'd done it all.

Well, almost all.

"You could take me back to bed."

Bedded Bliss

1

"SO, DO YOU HAVE any big plans for the weekend?"

Mallory turned away from her computer to reach for a file folder, hiding her expression of dismay. Maybe connecting via webcam with Bianca wasn't the best idea she'd had this morning. In fact, her store of good sense had been sparse all week. First, she'd failed to come up with a plan for luring the rock star, Brock Arsenal, to perform at the still-a-surprise-to-Bianca wedding, which was less than seventy-two hours away. Second, she'd scheduled a face-to-face call with the bride and was now struggling not to give away the secret. And third—and most shocking—she'd crazily consented to spend the weekend with Ajay Singh.

"Actually, yeah," she replied to Bianca's question.

Mallory had not reached thirty-two years of age without knowing quite a bit about her personal strengths and weaknesses. She was a relative loner, thanks to a lifelong battle with a phobia that made crowds hard to endure. She could speak over a half-dozen languages. She was comfortable living just about anywhere in the world, but in an attempt to avoid her former fiancé, she'd recently made Bianca's hometown, Tampa, Florida, her base of operations.

But at this particular moment, the most important thing she knew about herself was that she was a terrible liar.

Especially to Bianca, who was an unmitigated expert in all things related to human behavior. Telling the partial truth seemed the safest way to go.

Bianca was already bouncing in her seat at the idea that Mallory planned to abandon her sanctuary and actually get out of the house.

"Ooh! You have plans," she said with a squeal. "What's his name?"

Mallory pressed her lips tightly together. Could she admit this part? Out loud?

"Ajay. Ajay Singh."

Bianca's eyes widened into circles of pure disbelief.

"What? You can't!"

Mallory looked at the webcam, incredulous. This had been a difficult enough choice for her to make. She didn't need Bianca giving her a hard time about it—especially since the whole thing was on Bianca's behalf. Well, partially.

"He's Coop's boss and he's one of my biggest clients. He invited me to spend the weekend with him."

Bianca's voice raised an entire octave. "A weekend?"

"Well—" Mallory tried to conjure up a believable explanation that would not reveal their covert wedding plans, but Bianca cut her off.

"Wait, an entire weekend? Are you sure Ajay said the *whole* weekend?"

She waved her hand casually. "He needs help on some translation project he's working on. It's not a big deal."

Actually, it was a *huge* deal, but only because Mallory had chosen to make it so. She tried to remember the precise moment when she'd decided to seduce Ajay Singh. She figured it was right around the second time she'd caught him staring at her Tuesday night with his soulful, hypnotic jade-green eyes.

Bianca scooted closer to her laptop and glanced to the left and right, as if trying to make sure no one was within listening range. She and Coop would be heading back to Florida from Costa Rica later that afternoon, but from the background, Mallory could see they were still in their San Jose apartment. A huge window revealed the bright morning sky and the verdant slopes of the Andes in the distance.

"Any time Ajay asks a woman to spend more than twenty-four hours with him, it's a big deal," Bianca warned. "He's a player, Mal. World-class. I love him like a brother, but I've also known him for eight years. In all that time, he's never spent more than a night with any one woman. Even when we flew with him to Monte Carlo, he brought one girl on the plane and then had a different chick on his arm on the flight back."

Mallory gulped down her anticipation and hoped Bianca didn't notice. She was not surprised her friend was warning her off. Bianca had no way of knowing that the qualities that might make Ajay undesirable to a woman like Bianca—one who treasured loyalty and devotion above all else—made the man perfect for Mallory.

She'd just gotten off the roller-coaster ride of a so-called exclusive relationship, which had ended when her fiancé had told the world he was marrying someone else before he'd bothered to tell her. Ajay's proclivities away from commitment made him the ideal candidate for helping her get over the heartbreak.

Six months had passed since Carlo's betrayal, but his actions still haunted her. No matter what she saw when she looked in the mirror or heard from her very small circle of friends, she felt like the most undesirable woman in the universe.

But Ajay always made her feel beautiful. He was a shameless flirt, a devastatingly handsome charmer who gave her his full and undivided attention whenever their paths crossed. When they'd met again at the pizza parlor, he'd spent a considerable time attempting to seduce her with his eyes. In the crowded restaurant, she'd been too overwhelmed by her own anxiety to respond and spent the rest of the night kicking herself for not even giving the poor guy a smile.

She was tired of it—tired of living her life with little but regret and what-might-have-beens. She'd wasted so much on Carlo. She needed a boost to her confidence. She needed a man who would, temporarily, make her feel whole.

Then, maybe, she could move on—and just as Bianca warned, so would Ajay. She could walk into this weekend with no expectations except to thoroughly enjoy herself with a man who obviously knew how to please a woman. He might have the attention span of a gnat when it came to lovers, but he never had to look very hard to get one.

Mallory pasted on her most convincing expression of exasperation. "Ajay's only interested in me for business," she insisted. "We've known each other for a long time and he's never made a real pass at me. Why would this weekend be any different?"

Because this time, I'm going to be the one making the passes.

"Ajay doesn't pursue women who are spoken for," Bianca explained. "Until six months ago, you were with Carlo. Off-limits."

Mallory knew what her friend wanted to hear. She needed Mallory to declare that despite her unexpected breakup with the man she'd been engaged to for over three years, she was still out-of-bounds to Coop's playboy boss.

"I'm a big girl, Bianca," Mallory offered. "I know what I'm doing."

Bianca's eyes narrowed. "What project does he need help from you on? I could have Coop call him and ask for more details—"

Mallory cut her off. "I don't care about the particulars. I just want out of this condo."

Bianca's mouth curved in a compassionate frown. Mallory hated to use the sympathy card, but she had to keep her friend from digging too deeply. Coop's best friend, Leo, had forbidden them from talking with Bianca or Coop before they returned to Tampa, but Bianca had just finished the translating assignment Mallory had arranged for her in Central America, and with Mallory, business always came first. And besides, not having their post-assignment recap would have sparked Bianca's suspicions.

"Coop and I will be home early tomorrow morning," Bianca

replied. "We could do something fun this weekend. Maybe drive down to Captiva?"

"Thanks, Bianca," Mallory said, "but you need to spend some time with your family. In the meantime, I'm going to concentrate on keeping one of my biggest clients happy."

And hopefully, vice versa.

"Mal, you need to be careful. You're still hurting. You're vulnerable. Ajay isn't one to prey on defenseless women, but he's always thought you were beautiful and—"

"I'm not defenseless," Mallory argued, though the words sounded hollow after all she'd been through. "Admittedly, it would have been nice if Carlo had broken things off with me before he announced his upcoming marriage to the Italian newspapers, but I'm going to be fine."

"But you're not fine now," Bianca insisted. "You shouldn't run headlong from one bad situation into a worse one. Ajay's a great guy, Mal, but he's not...your type."

"And what is my type?" she asked, her voice snapping. "Let's see, I'm attracted to men who are incredibly intelligent, charismatic and, apparently, are users who will dump me the minute someone better comes along."

Bianca smirked. "Well, then maybe Ajay is your type."

Mallory snorted. "Exactly."

Mallory had met Ajay through Bianca and Coop. Their introduction had led him to hire Mallory's company, Tedesco Global Communications, to provide translators and interpreters for his maverick technology firm, Singh Systems, for which Coop was a primary designer. While on the arm of Carlo Brunori, her former fiancé, Mallory had encountered Ajay at charity events in Paris or high-profile holidays on the Isle of Capri. Even when she was supposed to be infinitely happy and in love, he'd caught her eye.

He caught every woman's eye. He epitomized tall, dark and handsome. Self-made and smarter than a few Nobel laureates, Ajay had an undeniable appeal.

But she'd had Carlo.

Or so she'd thought. Turned out, she'd never *had* him at

all—but he'd had her, wrapped around his slimy, double-dealing fingers.

"Don't worry about me," she told her friend. "Just tell me about Costa Rica."

Bianca filled her in on all the details of the assignment, which, as usual, had gone off without a hitch. As she spoke, Mallory completed the file for the American real estate firm who had hired Bianca to comb through the Costa Rican contracts with the firm's lawyers to ensure their multimillion-dollar deal went smoothly.

Bianca also hinted that she and Coop had had a little tropical adventure along the way, but Mallory didn't ask for details. She loved Bianca like the sister she'd never had, but she was in no state to endure yet another steamy tale of utter devotion and incredibly hot sex. Bianca and Coop had a million of them.

"So we'll see you tomorrow night?" Bianca asked.

Mallory pasted on her most innocent smile. "Of course."

"Mal, what aren't you telling me?"

"I'm just thinking about all the things I need to get done. I'm supposed to meet Ajay in an hour and I need to pack."

"Pack?"

Oops.

"Just a few things from the office."

And the bedroom.

Bianca turned the full force of her suspicious gaze on her, attempting, no doubt, to utilize her unique combination of intuition and street smarts to ferret out the truth. Like her friend, Mallory had lived all over the world, but she had never put herself out on the street long enough to get smart about it. In the battle to separate truth from fiction, Bianca was better armed.

Luckily, Mallory had more finesse with her computer.

Three keystrokes later and their connection started to zigzag.

"Bianca, you're breaking up. Fly safely. I'll see you tomorrow night," Mallory said and before her friend could question her further, the signal zapped.

Her apartment, yet again, was quiet as a tomb.

Mallory gazed at her luxury digs with disgust. Filled with furnishings from around the globe, the space was designed specifically to make clients confident in her abilities. Combining her working area with her living area made perfect sense—Mallory had no life outside of her business. Even her affair with Carlo had started when she'd acted as his interpreter during a weeklong marathon of business meetings between his Italian motorsports company and Japanese investors.

He'd been so irresistible to someone like her. She was brainy, but Carlo was clever. She appreciated sensual pursuits, but Carlo turned all things sexy into a full contact, no-holds-barred sport—from food to drink to gambling and of course, sex itself. He'd overwhelmed her, swept her off her feet. Made her forget, at least for brief spells, that public appearances gave her panic attacks that had, twice in her life, landed her in the hospital.

Carlo had seemed so understanding and accommodating. He'd never forced her to attend crowded premieres or schmooze through overpacked throngs while he glad-handed people whose money he loved to spend. He found quiet, out-of-the-way restaurants for them to share a meal, then took her back to their hotel, made love to her until she fell asleep, and burned off his excess of energy by partying the rest of his night with friends.

While he slept off his hangovers, she'd built her company into a premier supplier of language specialists. For three years, she'd allowed herself to believe that even though Carlo was her polar opposite in every way, their differences complemented one another. She'd provided the quiet he so desperately needed. He'd introduced her to the vast array of pleasurable pursuits available to those with enough clout and money to find them.

But he hadn't really needed her. He'd enjoyed having her, though, up until he'd found his new fiancée. Mallory couldn't bear to remember the nastiness he'd unleashed in not one, but two languages, once his new relationship had been revealed.

Thanks to Carlo, Mallory was now also fluent in heartbreak. The confidence she'd carried into the business world had been reduced to ashes. Since that night, she'd been operating on automatic, rarely leaving her condo, relying on repeat clientele rather than soliciting new business. She probably wouldn't have even gone out on Tuesday night, but knowing she might balk at a trip to a crowded pizzeria, Leo had told her his plan ahead of time.

Mallory couldn't say no. And she was glad she didn't, because one lingering stare from Ajay Singh had given her an idea that might turn her world upside down, but in the end, could have it spinning again for the first time in six long months.

Only three nights ago, she'd nearly melted under the heat of Ajay's not-so-furtive glances—and could only imagine what fire they might generate together with no pretense between them. So when both she and Ajay had been unsuccessful in contacting Brock Arsenal separately, he'd suggested they work together. He'd reserved a suite at the hotel where Arsenal was staying before his concert and invited her to join him.

She'd accepted—and hoped she was doing the right thing.

Or better yet, the wrong thing.

Trusting her own judgment no longer came easy. She'd loved Carlo and had believed he loved her. His declarations of undying devotion had sounded like poetry, though the echoes of his lies now clanged like a bell until her temples ached and her eyes burned. She needed to cleanse her memory of him. She was desperate to replace the feel of his hands and lips with those of a new man.

A better man.

A man who reveled in his capricious lifestyle and never pretended to be any more than he was.

And luckily for her, she was forty-five minutes away from spending the weekend with the perfect specimen.

She closed up her laptop and then went to her bedroom to toss the last of her personal items into her suitcase. She'd taken care of her toiletries, makeup and hair care products. She was all set until after the wedding on Sunday night. What she needed now was a wardrobe.

What exactly did one wear to seduce one of the world's most famous seducers?

To the old Mallory—the one who hadn't had her heart trampled on—this question would have sounded insane. She'd never gone out of her way to seduce anyone. She'd always clung to the fantasy of being swept away by a man. Sought-out and pursued, wined, dined and cascaded with flowers until she'd have no choice but to submit to his passionate whims.

Well, she'd been there, done that and ended up heartbroken and alone. And she'd wallowed long enough. Her closest friend was getting married this weekend and, damn it, she was going to enjoy the spectacle.

But to fully appreciate the event, she needed to leave the old Mallory behind. She needed to stop taking life and love so seriously—she needed to take her hardened heart into a temporary affair and come out the other end invigorated and renewed.

Red. She needed to wear red.

And with that critical decision made, she dug into her closet. In less than an hour, her transformation would begin—and poor Ajay Singh wouldn't know what hit him.

2

AJAY NEARLY dropped his bag. Never mind that it contained a state-of-the-art laptop, a prototype cell phone that utilized radiotelegraphy technology or the expandable flat screen monitor his R&D team wanted him to test this weekend. His toys could break into a thousand pieces and the aftermath wouldn't slam him nearly as hard as witnessing Mallory Tedesco sashay across the hotel lobby in a hot red dress.

All moisture evaporated from his mouth. He might have started to pant if the overattentive manager hadn't just appeared beside him with an ice-cold drink.

"Sir, is there anything else we can get you?"

He gulped down two mouthfuls of tea. "Is my room ready?"

Why in the name of Krishna had he arranged for a suite with two bedrooms? He certainly hadn't suggested this weekend get-together with hope for a tryst with Mallory—not after the cool reception she'd given him Tuesday night. But a woman did not put on a dress that shade or shape—body-hugging, thigh-high and with a neckline that didn't reveal an inch of skin and yet showed everything of importance—without intending to seduce the man she was coming to meet.

Unless she only intended to torture him. If that was her plan, she'd already succeeded.

"I can take you upstairs immediately," the manager replied.

"Then, no, there's nothing else you can get me. All I need is coming my way."

Mallory, who had not spotted him when she entered the lobby, made eye contact. Her step, so bold and swinging until that moment, faltered. Ajay gave her a nod and in that split second a bellman dashed to her side.

He doubted he'd need to tip the guy for the instantaneous service. Mallory had provided him with what might be the biggest payoff of his entire morning. The normally cool, endlessly serious woman Ajay had always considered off-limits had drawn the attention of every single man in the lobby—and quite a few of the women. Luckily, the boutique hotel was not large. He didn't want competition.

He took one last sip of the glacial tea, handed it off to the manager and then started toward Mallory. "Mallory, you look— I'm afraid I don't have adequate words."

That was a lie. He had a whole cadre of adequate words. *Hot. Sexy. Spectacular. Delicious. Amazing.*

Her lashes fluttered low. "I hope that's a good thing."

Ajay felt a rumble low in his belly, like hunger, but inherently more powerful. Food he could have any old time. What he wanted was a bite of Mallory—which, unfortunately, was not unlike craving forbidden fruit.

"You're going to eclipse the bride if you're not careful."

Her laughter was light and just a tad cynical. "Your reputation as a practiced charmer is not apocryphal, I see."

He pressed his hand to his chest, as if she'd wounded him. "I have a reputation?"

"You do, and you know it. I wouldn't be surprised if you were the one who started the rumors in the first place."

He leaned in close, intending his reply for her ears only. "For a woman who hardly knows me, you seem to know me fairly well."

"And I hope to know you better by the end of this weekend," she murmured.

Had he not been so near, he might not have believed she'd be so daring. Coupled with the intoxicating scent of her perfume—a light fragrance laced with deep, warm amber and sharp, exotic jasmine—he wondered if this was the same Mallory Tedesco he'd known for three years or if her body had been snatched by some sensual alien creature.

Though she usually wore her thick hair pulled loosely away from her face in a simple, no-nonsense style, today she'd let the brunette waves flow over her shoulders and down her back, which he'd just realized had none of the red material that covered her so perfectly in front. Her skin was bare, tanned and perfectly curved, leading to a backside he wanted to wrap his hands around so badly his fingers ached. She turned again and looked directly into his eyes—just as she had Tuesday night, only this time, she actually seemed to welcome his stare. Her smoky, dark eyes and her cranberry-stained mouth begged for his attention—and Ajay wasn't one to let a woman beg.

He held out his arm, his muscles twitching in anticipation. "So, ready to work?"

Her tongue darted out and smoothed over her lips. Again, his grip on his bag loosened as blood rushed away from all of his extremities except the one in his slacks. Had she come here to help him lure Brock Arsenal to sing at Bianca and Coop's wedding or to torment him to madness?

"I suppose." With breathless nonchalance, she slid her palm over his biceps.

Air released from his lungs with a sizzling hiss. He thought, though he wasn't sure, that he spied her quick smile. She was enjoying tempting him and he would have bet his portfolio that a woman like her knew better than to play with fire.

They followed the manager to the private elevator that led to one of two suites atop the only five-star hotel in Tampa's historic district. Brock Arsenal had already booked the larger one. He and Mallory would share the other.

"Are you sure he's staying here tonight?" she asked.

The guest relations manager, who'd joined them in the lift, glanced at them, surprised. If they followed usual protocol, the hotel would try to keep Arsenal's presence at their hotel a secret. The last thing they needed was to be overrun with fans.

"According to his concert promoter," he replied. He'd worked all week to find a connection to the rock star, and a contact with the group that was sponsoring his appearance was the best he'd come up with. He had little information beyond the guy's hotel, however, but Ajay figured that was enough. He'd certainly made more out of less.

"Are you admirers of Mr. Arsenal?" the manager asked.

Mallory turned on her sweetest smile. The guy puffed up a half a foot above his somewhat diminutive stature. "Absolutely," she said, tugging Ajay slightly closer. "He's our favorite performer."

Ajay suddenly wished he'd kept that iced tea. The inside of his mouth had dried and he would need replenishment if he was going to do what she was tempting him to—kiss the breath out of her the moment they were alone.

But no. He couldn't. Mallory was off-limits. She was Bianca's boss and Coop's friend. He knew her only as a business associate, but despite his inability to keep from flirting with her whenever she was around, she was not the type of woman one made love to and then tossed aside. Ajay wasn't into commitment. He avoided romantic entanglements at all costs. And worse, she was on the rebound. Definitely dangerous territory. For both of them.

He'd met her idiot former fiancé, Carlo Brunori, whose recent engagement to a French socialite indicated that he'd dumped Mallory for someone not half as beautiful but infinitely better connected. Ajay had never quite understood what Mallory saw in the man in the first place. Sure, he was Italian and a decent businessman, but every time Ajay ran into him, he was late-night clubbing with kids half his age or sunning on nude beaches in St. Tropez while Mallory was back at their villa running her business.

He'd found the pairing unusual, but as a live-and-let-live

kind of guy, he'd said nothing. Mallory was a friend of a friend. Nothing more. Not his concern.

Until now. Now, she was concerning every inch of him.

When the elevator dinged on the top floor, Ajay caught her staring. Just like when the roles were reversed at the pizzeria, she held his gaze. But unlike that meeting, this time, she lowered her lashes seductively and then winked.

Winked?

She was making a play for him. In a big way. Unless he was mistaken—and about these things, Ajay was never wrong.

The manager opened the double doors to the suite. The decor combined the dark, paneled wood favored in historic districts and light, breezy furnishings that fit the relaxed Florida lifestyle. The center room was a spacious combination of living room and kitchen, with an intimate table set for two near the balcony. To the left was one bedroom with a massive, decadent bathroom replete with garden tub. To the right, a second bedroom and bath with a quad-headed shower. Ajay's brain was determining precisely where he'd point those pulses of water on Mallory's naked body when he remembered they weren't yet alone.

Their luggage was delivered. A hotel valet, an older man who greeted them with a quick bow, placed the suitcases in their rooms, filled their ice bucket and asked if they'd like him to unpack. They declined. Neither of them had brought much—and Ajay wasn't sure if this was a blessing or a curse.

Mallory kept her hand on his arm while the guest relations manager showed them the rest of the amenities, from the wine bar stocked with Ajay's preferred vintages to a selection of gourmet snacks in the refrigerator and sumptuous robes embroidered not with the hotel's logo, but with a stylized bull for him and a chic scorpion for her.

She let go of him long enough to run her hand over the plush microfiber knit fabric. "That's my sun sign," she said. "Scorpio. How did you know?"

"I do my research," he replied.

When the hotel had offered the service, he'd spared only

a few seconds' consideration before deciding a personalized wrap would be a nice gift for a woman who'd been a steady supplier to his business for quite a few years. Now he realized how personal the gesture seemed—and he wasn't sorry.

He couldn't resist touching the robe himself and the incredible softness only enhanced his need to graze his fingers over her skin. But he held back. He'd come to the hotel with Mallory for one reason—to convince Brock Arsenal to play his most famous ballad at Bianca and Coop's wedding. And yet Ajay had arranged for them to share a suite rather than opting for separate rooms. Again, he hadn't spared the decision much consideration, but he now realized that his subconscious had acted where his strong sense of self-preservation had not.

He'd been unable to keep his mind off Mallory since Tuesday night. He hadn't intended to seduce her, but if she was pushing him in that direction, he did not have the strength of will to resist. What man would?

"According to your astrological sign," he said, fingering the red raised embroidery that would nestle against her breast once she donned the soft robe, "you are passionate, exciting and obsessive. True or false?"

She pulled the robe away from him, and then seemed to catch her reflexive move and stopped short, instead rubbing the downy fabric against her cheek. "I didn't realize a man like you would put stock in such things."

She'd replied, but she'd given him no real answer at all.

"It's my cultural background. No one in India makes a move without first consulting their astrologer."

She laughed. "You didn't get where you are by following the dictates of the stars."

This much was true. He was entertained by astrology, but not a slave to it the way his mother seemed to be. And his grandparents. And to some degree, even his very reasonable, inherently logical twin brother. "Perhaps I should have. Maybe then I'd have been prepared for being alone in a spacious hotel room with you in this incredible red dress."

She looked around, her surprise that the valet and the

manager had both left evident on her face. He, on the other hand, had noticed the moment they'd discreetly departed. The entire atmosphere of the room had shifted and though daylight streamed through the bank of windows on the west wall, he couldn't imagine a space that was more conducive to sex.

Two beds, each more plush and inviting than the other. Two bathrooms equipped with accoutrements to enhance lovemaking. A stocked wine bar. Loungewear that encouraged them to strip down to nothing and wrap themselves in its decadent softness.

How he was going to stop himself from coming on to her was a mystery. And one he wasn't sure he wanted to solve.

Their mutual friendship with Coop and Bianca notwithstanding, he couldn't see any problem with sleeping with Mallory. She'd seen him on the town. She knew he did not make promises to women beyond pledging that a night in his bed would be something they'd never forget. He never took phone numbers. He never played the role of pursuer. When a woman came on to him, he took notice and if she was attractive, entertaining and preferably had enough financial resources so that she would not bother with his, he followed through.

Mallory's beauty was undeniable. Expressive eyes. Supple, dark skin. Long hair that reminded him of sable or mink. She wasn't loquacious by any means, but what she said mattered. Her business acumen had made her quite successful—she had too much money of her own to be sniffing after his.

But in the past, she'd never looked at him twice. Even on Tuesday night, she'd hardly spoken a word, much less flirted.

What had changed?

She sauntered across the suite to what would be his bed and laid her scorpion-branded robe against the bull-embroidered one the valet had placed across the chocolate-brown duvet. The stark whiteness of the material against the rich color of the bedspread conjured images in his mind of how she'd look with the pearly fabric against her olive skin. When her eyes met his again, he couldn't help but wonder if she was considering stripping down right then and there.

But sadly, her nudity would mean the removal of that spectacular red dress.

"What time does Brock Arsenal arrive at the hotel?"

Ajay blinked, then forced his brain to process the information she'd asked for. He returned to the main room and retrieved his bag, from which he took the prototype cell phone. Several taps later and he had the itinerary he'd put together.

"His flight lands at ten. He performed last night in Atlanta, and then spent today with his sister and her kids in the city. I imagine that once he arrives here, he'll either be looking for a good night's sleep or a wild rock 'n' roll party."

"We could provide the party," she suggested, her gaze sweeping around the suite. "The manager would set it all up if you throw enough cash around."

He'd actually considered that option, but now disliked the idea altogether. He suddenly wanted this room to be for him and Mallory alone.

"Maybe we'll swing an invitation to whatever he's doing."

"Have you met him before?"

Ajay drifted toward her, standing at what he hoped was a safe distance in the threshold between the living area and his bedroom. She tossed out her sultry-voiced questions as she explored, running her fingers over the thick fabric of the drapes before she dragged the curtains closed against the midmorning glare and threw the room into golden shadows.

"Once," Ajay replied, his throat tight. "Years ago. I don't think we actually exchanged names. I was in London and someone in our dinner party invited him to join our table. I don't believe he spoke to me. He was much more interested in flirting with my date."

She hummed as if in understanding. "I've heard that about him."

Again, she passed by the bed and smoothed her hand over the robe embroidered with her sun sign. "I read a blog on the Internet that called him the ultimate poacher."

"I read that article," Ajay said with a snort. "I believe there was another adjective in front of that noun."

The blogger had actually dubbed the man a "pussy poacher" because of his proclivity for stealing women away from other men.

"I didn't think I needed to be crass," Mallory said silkily, lowering herself onto the edge of the bed and turning so that her sinfully long legs tucked against the mattress.

"The word doesn't always have to be crass," he replied.

Had the valet turned up the thermostat before he left?

"It usually is. In my experience, which I admit—" she met his gaze boldly "—isn't extensive."

But his was. Oh, boy, was his experience ever extensive. And yet, he suddenly felt uneasy and unsure, but in the most interesting way.

"I've found it all depends on how it is said," he claimed. "And to whom. And when."

She slid down onto the mattress and petted the plush robe, much like he wanted to pet her in precisely the part of her anatomy they were now skirting around discussing.

He couldn't do this, could he? Seduce Bianca's friend? Right before the wedding?

"Show me," she said.

"Excuse me?"

She actually crooked her finger and beckoned him toward the bed. "Show me how that word can be used to seduce a woman. Must take a man with incredibly honed skills of seduction to pull that off."

This was a challenge. A gauntlet thrown. A glove slapped across the face.

He shouldn't. He had no business swinging in this playground.

And yet, he couldn't resist falling to his knees at her feet.

3

MALLORY REMINDED HERSELF to breathe, but the conscious directive from her brain to her lungs did not seem to jump-start her respiratory system. The minute that Ajay knelt at her feet, a rush of air caught her unaware. She gasped.

"First, a man can't say the word too loudly."

His voice was the barest whisper. His breath skittered up her arm as he took her hand, his face level with her breasts. His gaze lingered on her curves and her nipples immediately tightened against the snug material of her dress. She'd opted not to wear a bra with this backless number and the decision was at once foolish and brilliant beyond measure. He eyed the twin outlines of her arousal hungrily, then swept his insatiable gaze down to her legs.

He touched her ankle. As if fascinated by the curve of her calf, he traced a light path up her leg, lingering at the sensitive spot behind her knee.

"If I whisper, you have to lean in to hear me," he murmured.

She did as he requested, shifting so that her head was only inches from his mouth. His hot breath curled around the shell of her ear, igniting a wildfire of sensation against her skin.

"I also find," he continued, nuzzling his nose against

her hair, "that the word sounds best when delivered with a promise—the kind a man can't help but keep."

He pressed his lips against her neck. Electric sensations shot through her, an instantaneous awareness that centered in the part of her body he was talking about—and yet, so far, not mentioning at all.

"What kind of promise?" she dared ask.

His fingers on her leg had now ascended past her knee and lingered at the hem of her dress. He teased the edge of the fabric, tracing back and forth, but never crossing.

Every couple of strokes, he paused to kiss her, dropping his head slightly so that his mouth inched from her shoulder across her collarbone to the center of her sternum, directly above the swell of her breasts.

"Something like, 'I'm going to slip my fingers into your sweet…'" he whispered the word and the popping *P* and sibilant *S*'s made her quiver. "Does that sound crass?"

His hand continued to tantalize, skimming at her skin, heightening her awareness so that she could not stop herself from imagining what it would feel like if he pushed passed her hem and fulfilled his pledge.

"No," she said. "It's sexy."

When he licked his lips, she felt a swipe of moisture an inch above her nipple. She nearly cried out.

"It's a sweet word. Slick. Slide. Sex. It all works to seduce the senses."

She couldn't stop her knees from parting, ready for him to make good on his promises.

"Yes," she said.

She was answering his question. She was egging him on. Her sex pulsed for his touch. She scooted forward, meeting his tantalizing fingers halfway.

"What if I told you your—" he repeated the word again "—is warm and wet?"

"I'd ask…how you could possibly know," she replied.

He chuckled, his mouth vibrating against her throat as he

kissed his way up to her ear. His hand drew nearer to her center. He leaned forward, nudging completely between her legs.

"A man knows," he said, kissing along her jawline. "I can hear your heartbeat. I can hear the blood rushing down into those luscious pink lips."

"Which lips?"

He answered with a crash of his mouth against hers. On fire, Mallory spiked her hands into his hair and kissed him back. Their tongues tangled, battled and won little victories of sensation and flavor. He tasted like tea and sugar, but she drank him in like pure, sweet rum.

When he drew aside her thong, she remembered his original pledge.

"I don't make many promises," Ajay whispered, "but the ones I make, I keep."

His words elicited an instant wave of moisture, hot drops that seared her thighs and intensified his measured, deliberate touch.

"Then keep it," she begged.

"I will," he replied, pressing his fingertip momentarily against her clitoris. "In my own time. My own way."

He held all the cards, possessed all the power—and Mallory did not care. He parted her flesh, capturing the moisture pearling from her sex and swirling it into a building wave. Then he found her clit again, manipulating it until she panted for breath.

"Ajay," she said. "Oh, God."

"Say the word, Mallory," he said.

"What?"

"Say the word. Sing it in my ear. Confess it to me."

When she complied, he pressed a finger inside her, jolting her with sensations she had not realized her body so desperately craved.

"Again," he commanded.

She did and once more, he rewarded her, deepening his strokes, increasing his tempo.

She clutched at his shoulders, certain she was falling into an abyss of pleasure.

"Once more," he goaded.

The third time, he pushed her over the edge. He lengthened his reach, quickened his pace. In what seemed like seconds, she was lost in a whirlpool of ecstasy. Her climax, so concentrated, burst from deep within her. He milked every last sensation from her body, kissing her long and hard until she could again see in sharp focus and the mere act of breathing did not singe the inside of her lungs.

Then, slowly, he put her thong back in place and tugged down the hem of her dress.

She stretched out across the bed, her body thrumming. For an instant, she wondered what he would do now. This wasn't supposed to happen like this—so quickly, so unexpectedly.

Only that was a lie. From the donning of the red dress, every word and action she'd thrown his way since they met in the lobby had led them here.

The bed shifted as he lay down beside her.

She swallowed.

"Convinced?" he asked.

She managed a nod.

"Words are just words. We give them power."

Mallory could offer no argument—at least, not one she could formulate with any degree of sense. She had not come to him for philosophy. She'd come to him for sex. And he not only knew it, he'd wasted no time in complying.

The question was, what next?

For the first time, she realized that up until now, she had not considered the aftermath. She'd focused on the man. Both sexy and sexual, she imagined that any woman who was in his presence for any amount of time knew that Ajay appreciated beauty and did not believe in denial. Now that she no longer had reason to forswear what she desperately wanted, she was drawn to his hedonism. He'd presented her with a priceless gift—an orgasm that had cost her nothing. One that did not, in the moment of release, give him a piece of her soul.

"Ajay," she started, but what was she going to say? *Thanks for the big O? I got what I came for, now it's time to talk about that rock star?*

He tilted an eyebrow at her. "Yes?"

Laughter burbled up inside her. Never in her life had she put herself into such a ridiculous yet liberating position. She attempted to cover her mouth to hold the hilarity at bay, but he caught her wrist.

"Don't hold back, Mallory. If you want to laugh, then do it."

With Ajay, she didn't need much encouragement. In seconds, she was giggling like a schoolgirl, blushing furiously and attempting to cover her face with her hands, which he did not allow. He captured them in his and brushed a light kiss across each row of knuckles.

"I don't know what got into me."

"Liar," he said, pressing his mouth to the pulse points on each of her wrists.

"Okay, okay," she confessed, dragging in a deep breath to quell her laughter. "I came here this weekend intending to seduce you."

"You succeeded."

"Not exactly. Seduction usually results in mutual pleasure. You haven't gotten anything out of the deal just yet."

He smirked. "Yes, well, the day is still young. And not that I mind being seduced, but I am infinitely curious to know why you chose me."

"Fishing for compliments?" she asked, hoping her saucy reply would keep him from pressing further. She could see no way to confess the truth—that she'd wanted him because of his experience and reputation for keeping his liaisons short and uncomplicated.

"I won't turn those down, but no. If you won't confess to why me, then at least…why now?"

That question was just as bad.

"I don't suppose you'd believe me if I said weddings get me excited?"

He smiled. "Of anyone else, I might buy it, but you are not exactly an excitable woman, Mallory. Or spontaneous."

"I can be spontaneous," she lied.

He merely lifted an eyebrow. One of these days, she was going to work on her ability to hide the truth.

"I suppose you heard about me and Carlo," she said, resigned to digging up the ugly reality.

He turned his head to the side and tsked, as if the speaking of Carlo's name required him to spit in response. "That was months ago. And for the record, he didn't deserve you."

"Thanks," she whispered. "But those months have been tough. And Tuesday night, I don't know, I felt this connection with you. Didn't you?"

His grin shifted from amused to wicked. "What I felt on Tuesday was an overwhelming desire to strip you naked and explore every crevice and curve of your body. But then, I've pretty much felt that every time we've run into each other."

"Now you're the liar," she said.

His expression froze with utmost seriousness. "No, Mallory, I'm not."

Her chest clenched. Ajay may be a playboy, but she knew he was also painfully, unequivocally honest. He made his rounds with the ladies, but from what she gathered, none of them ended up with a broken heart or dashed expectations like she had with Carlo. Ajay was clear and up-front—he wasn't looking for a relationship. Up until now, she'd never once wondered why that was.

"I've always wanted you, too," she said.

But again, he caught her. "No, you haven't. And that's okay," he said with a chuckle. "I'm not offended. Bianca always said you were the smartest woman she knew. But if there's one thing I'm well versed in, aside from electronic circuitry, it's women. You stared me down Tuesday, but not because you wanted me. You were terrified I'd do something unthinkable. Like come on to you. Or worse, touch you. Then this morning, you did everything in your power to make sure I touched you, in the most intimate way possible—which I should mention, I enjoyed very much and would like to do again at the earliest opportunity. But I'd be remiss if I didn't ask again—what's changed?"

She considered sitting up, but she did not wish to break the spell that entwined them on the bed. Staring into his jade-green eyes, speaking in hushed tones about such private topics, was a rare and wonderful experience. She watched him scan her face like one of his advanced computer systems—his gaze sensitive to every twitch in her cheek, every blink of her lashes. He wanted to know. The fact that he cared about what had brought her to this point struck her hard.

"I'm tired of living life in a shell," she admitted.

He pushed aside a strand of hair that had fallen across her cheek. "I can imagine that would be a very cramped existence."

"You have no idea."

He kissed the tip of her nose. The gesture was so sweet, so innocent—so in contrast to what they'd just done.

"You're right…I don't have any idea," he said, his mouth turned downward in a pensive frown. "But there's a danger to living your life out loud all the time, too. You can't hear yourself enough to figure out who you really are or what you really want. You take what's offered and ignore the consequences. But sooner or later, it catches up to you."

His confession surprised her. "That's…very contemplative."

He laughed. "Yes, well, I've been known to have a deep thought from time to time. I try to avoid it if I can, of course."

"Yeah, who doesn't?"

This time, when he chuckled, she joined in. The situation was ridiculous and absurd—a woman like her coming on to a man like him—and yet, things had gone according to plan. Her body still hummed with the aftermath of her orgasm and the warmth in his gaze only reinvigorated her libido. She wanted more from him—but more of what, she couldn't precisely say. More lovemaking? Definitely. More intimate conversation?

Why not? But what else could there be between them, especially once the wedding was over?

She reminded herself that she'd achieved exactly what she'd hoped to by coming here with seduction on her mind. She'd hoped that Ajay would respond to her flirtations, get turned on, have sex with her and make her feel desirable after so many months of feeling like garbage Carlo had tossed away. Her ex had found someone better—someone with no fear, someone he could bring into his crazy, superficial world without worrying that she'd have a panic attack or say something pedantic in the midst of conversations about the best wines, the hottest clubs or the latest fashions. She could converse about those topics, yes, but she could also discuss the latest political uprising in South America, expound on the economic impact of a new trade agreement or argue about the symbolism and imagery in ancient art.

Would that kind of woman appeal to a man like Ajay any more than it had Carlo?

Given his reputation, did it matter?

He slipped his hand onto her waist, splaying his fingers possessively over her hips.

"Who do you think I am, Mallory?"

The question caught her completely unaware.

"I think you're a man who appreciates women," she said.

He considered her words, as if searching for an untruth, but then gave a little nod.

"And I think you're a man who cares about living life to the fullest," she added.

Again, a nod.

"And I also think you're a man who has a raging erection and who wouldn't mind a little relief."

To this, he answered with a groan.

She'd made the comment half to distract him, half because she was dying to know if the rigid muscle pressing against her leg was as long, thick and hard as intimated by the pressure on her leg. The minute she slid her hand between them, she couldn't fight the urge to explore—maybe return the favor he'd so recently given her. She worked his belt free, unbuttoned his waistband and released the zipper.

"Mallory, you don't have—"

"Ajay, the only thing we have to do this weekend is get Brock Arsenal to sing at the wedding," she said, squeezing her fingers past the waistband of his briefs. "And he's not due for hours. What if until then, we do not what we have to, but what we want to?"

She wrapped her palm around him and gave a little squeeze, which elicited another tortured groan.

"Mallory, I love the way you think."

She hummed her appreciation. "Good. Then I think I'm going to love driving you mad."

4

IN TEN SECONDS FLAT, Ajay forgot every preconceived notion he'd ever formed about Mallory Tedesco. He'd been wholly mistaken when he interpreted her intelligence as bookishness and her coolness as snobbery. He'd opted to ignore her wit and beauty and instead pretend she was not a woman he'd ever desire.

And yet, every time their paths had crossed, he'd felt that wholly unfamiliar tug of wanting something he could not have.

Unaccustomed to dealing with anything in his life that he could not, with a bit of work and ingenuity, possess, he'd simply told himself that she was untouchable. Unlike Brock Arsenal, Ajay did not poach another man's woman. Then her fiancé had gone and dumped her.

And once she'd decided to have Ajay, he had no means to resist.

Every single nerve ending in his body worshipped her, starting with the sensitive skin of his sex, which had swelled to full length under her touch. She ringed his flesh with her fingers and stroked, drawing the pressure down to the hilt and then tugging to his head until he had no blood left in any other part of his body. With her other hand, she flicked open the buttons of his shirt so she could bathe his chest with butterfly-light kisses that contrasted against her commanding hold on his cock. She was a study in divergence. Shy, yet bold. Beautiful, yet self-conscious. Cool, and at the same time utterly at ease with giving him pleasure.

He wriggled out of his shirt, then did what he could to remove her dress and gain access to the rest of her. As he loosened the zipper on her side and then tugged down the shoulders to bare her breasts, Mallory kicked his pants aside, leaving him naked while her red dress bunched in her middle, exposing a bit of her thong panties and the luscious, intimate folds he'd only begun to explore.

She moved to yank the dress off, but he stopped her.

"Don't," he begged, taking a moment to appreciate how the material buoyed breasts tipped with dusky nipples and amazingly round areolae. "I love this on you."

"It's not covering much right now," she said, her voice almost shy.

He climbed to his knees on the mattress, and then had her do the same. He lifted the material of the dress so that her bottom was completely bare and her sex peeked from behind the tiny triangle of her lingerie.

"It's covering just enough."

He wrapped his arms around her waist and bent his head to take her nipple into his mouth. She arched her back and slid her hands into his hair, tugging slightly as his efforts intensified. Judging by the increasing tempo of her coos and moans, she liked this. Her breasts were sensitive to his tongue, his teeth, his touch. He used all three until she was grinding her sex against his, pleading with her body for release.

He laid her down atop the duvet, then hurried to the bathroom to retrieve his overnight kit. He tossed it onto the nightstand and then, at the edge of the bed, stopped to watch her watching him.

Her eyes, dark as ebony, were wide with anticipation. Her lips were slightly open, her tongue darting out at intervals to replenish the moisture she lost with each panting breath. She'd left the dress on as he'd requested, and the sight of her nipples, pink from his pleasuring, made his cock twitch with renewed need.

"You're so beautiful, Mallory."

"You keep saying it and I'll just have to believe you."

He went to the foot of the bed, climbing on at her feet, eyeing the pantie he'd have to remove before he could have what he most desired.

"Why don't I just show you how hot you are?"

He hooked a finger beneath the side of her thong and with a slowness that tortured him as much as it did her, he dragged the material down her leg. Once it was tossed aside, he lifted her left leg and kissed the arch of her foot, the curve of her ankle, the tight muscle of her calf. At her knees, he lingered, filling himself with the salty sweetness of her skin, feeding off the tremors in her flesh that gauged the building pressure of her need. When she spread her legs, giving him a view of his ultimate destination, he had to use all his self-control to continue his lazy path.

The moment he finally tasted what he'd previously only touched, he lost his mind in the flavor of her. Hot and wet, his tongue delved deeply into the folds of her flesh, his nostrils flaring with the scent of her arousal. Light-headed with want, he feasted and explored, learning her as intimately as any man could know a woman—memorizing the way she bucked when he flicked his tongue in one particular direction or how she moaned when he pulled gently at her flesh with his teeth.

"Ajay, please," she said.

He looked up and saw that she clutched the sides of the pillows in tight fists.

"I can't resist," he said, swirling his tongue around her rigid clit.

"You're torturing me. I don't…want to come…again."

"There's no limit on them, you know. You can come now," he teased, tonguing the tiny nub until she whimpered. "And then again. And then again."

She grabbed him by the cheeks and made defying her impossible. Chuckling, he stretched out over her, donned a condom and then pressed his erection against her, teasing her sensitive flesh with the lubricated tip.

She groaned with impatience and wrapped her legs around his waist. His body slid into hers with a burst of sensation. In the split second Ajay took to savor the moment, she started to unravel.

The contraction of her muscles around him marked the beginning of her release. She clutched at his back with her fingernails. He knew one thrust would take her over the top, but now that he was inside her, he wanted to slow down. He tensed every muscle and willed his heartbeat to slow, kissing her in one long, desperate attempt to gain time to catch up.

But her hungry mouth on his undid his resolve. In seconds, he was thrusting into her. She took what he gave, bucking into him, increasing the friction, fueling the pace. When he came, the explosion rocked him. He grabbed her hands, held on tight and rode the wave of pleasure until he couldn't hold himself up any longer. He collapsed beside her, kissing her intently until their breathing regulated and the sweat that covered their bodies had cooled in the circulating air.

"Wow," he said.

She smiled. "I bet you say that to all the girls."

He matched her grin, but said nothing. Had he experienced anything so spectacular lately? He couldn't recall. When he was young, the semi-anonymous sex he'd enjoyed had been awesome. But lately, most orgasms had been followed by a hollow sensation in the pit of his stomach. He'd filled the void with idle chatter, food, alcohol or more sex.

With Mallory, however, he felt full. Her confessions about Carlo and her guarded lifestyle awakened protective instincts he hadn't realized he possessed. Her sexual curiosity fed his need to explore every aspect of physical pleasure. He had feasted on her, body and soul, and was sated beyond measure. His brain whirled with the intoxication of her flavors. And while he was certain he'd want more sex as soon as his body recovered, for the moment, he was perfectly content to lie in her arms until nightfall.

Mallory, however, had other ideas. After a few moments, she shifted so that he had no choice but let her go. She clutched at the robe barely hanging on to the corner of the mussed bed and threw it over herself while she dashed into the bathroom. Suddenly chilly, he grabbed his own robe and slipped it over his shoulders long enough to cut through the living room, clean up in the other bathroom, and then grab her overnight bag.

When she did not emerge in five minutes, he knocked.

"Mallory, are you okay?"

She opened the door. Her expression was a mixture of emotions—too many for him to sort. He saw heavy-lidded eyes that shone with satisfaction, cheeks red from either exertion or embarrassment and mouth swollen not only from his teeth, but from hers, which were even now gnawing at her lips nervously.

"I'm not entirely sure," she said.

"Talk to me."

Had he ever said that to a lover before? Not once, but twice? In the same day?

"I'm a little shocked by how easily that went," she confessed.

He coaxed her into his arms. "You can't fight chemistry."

"I was desperate," she said with a sigh.

He nearly choked. "So you're saying you would have slept with just any guy today?"

"No! That's not what I meant. I wasn't that desperate—only desperate for you."

He snuggled closer, loving how he could smell his cologne mingling with the scent of her perfume, her shampoo, her. "That's more like it."

"But you have to know, Ajay. I don't expect anything—"

"Well, you should," he said, cutting her off. He didn't want to lay out any ground rules. For the first time in a long while, Ajay wanted real spontaneity in his love life. What he'd had before had become rote. Meet willing woman. Have date. Have sex. Say goodbye. Rinse and repeat.

"You should not only expect more of what we just did," he

continued, "you should demand it. And I promise to do my very best to meet your high standards of performance."

As he'd hoped, she laughed. Tension left her body and she curved fully into his arms, pressing her cheek against his chest. Could she hear how his heart skipped a beat?

"And here I thought you were an expert negotiator," she mused.

He pushed her back far enough so she could see his face. "Who says I'm not going to get something spectacular out of the deal, as well?"

"I'll do my best," she assured him, lifting her chin so that he could not resist kissing her.

Yet even as their lips melded and their tongues clashed, he wondered if her best might just kill him—or worse.

Like make him fall in love.

5

FOR LUNCH, Ajay ordered room service and fed her grilled lobster from a tiny silver fork and chocolate-covered strawberries from his delectable fingers. He kept their flutes of chilled champagne filled and then offered her a deep muscle massage at his skilled hands. Now, as she sat on the marble edge of the garden tub finishing off the last of her bubbly, he drew her bath.

The scent of lavender enriched the steamy air. Mallory untied her robe and pressed the cold glass to her chest. She might have pinched herself to see if she was actually awake, but the ache between her thighs assured her she was not sleeping. She knew all about dream sex—and what she'd shared with Ajay had been very, very real.

She'd come to the hotel this morning with seduction as her goal and she'd accomplished that, and more. This wasn't a big surprise. She'd constructed her whole life around working hard for satisfying rewards. She rarely set her mind to something without achieving it in the end—a fact about herself she'd forgotten in the maelstrom of emotions stirred by her breakup.

But now that she remembered, she couldn't help but question her relationship with Carlo. Had she really wanted him? She certainly hadn't tried very hard to keep him. She'd enjoyed his attention, and she'd liked the lifestyle he'd introduced her to, but she'd never embraced it. She'd preferred to work when he was playing and sleep while he was partying. Surrounded by underlings who took their jobs seriously, Carlo did not have to do much to keep his family's automotive company running. Mallory, on the other hand, was very hands-on.

In the warm aftermath of making love to Ajay, a man who wanted nothing from her, she realized that she and the man she'd nearly married had nothing in common.

Before she finished off the last swallow of her champagne, she lifted the glass to toast the poor woman who was stuck with him now. Mallory had dodged a bullet that would have, slowly and painfully, leaked the last of her life from her soul.

"I hope you like it hot," Ajay said after dipping his hand into the tub.

"Absolutely." She stood and removed her robe, loving how his eyes darkened as the soft material pooled at her feet.

Too bad Mallory couldn't have Ajay in her life beyond this weekend—they seemed much more compatible. Similar work ethics. The same friends. A desire to travel and explore the world, but not at the expense of the companies they'd worked so hard to build.

But she wasn't going to fool herself. Ajay wasn't a man who craved commitment and in the end, Mallory wanted that more than anything else. Her parents had been married for more than thirty-five years. She was certain Bianca and Coop's union would last just as long, if they didn't fall off a mountain or drown while scuba diving the Great Barrier Reef first. She would not ruin this weekend by asking Ajay for something he couldn't give.

"Ready?" he said. He flipped off his robe and climbed inside, hissing when the hot water met his dark skin.

"You're joining me?"

"A tub this size?" he asked, folding his arms behind his head. Even at his height, he had no trouble stretching out in the tub, leaving plenty of room for her. "Seems a terrible waste of water and foam if we don't both indulge."

His smile was lethal—pearly white against decadent burnt-umber skin, his jade-green eyes sparkling with a mischievous lust for life that proved both irresistible and infectious. She stepped into the water, her foot instantly registering the searing temperature.

"Yikes," she said.

He took her hand and guided her the rest of the way. Less than two hours ago, he'd seen her from every intimate angle possible and yet, his expression filled with appreciation as if this was the first time. He drank her in, making each movement a mini-seduction. When she finally settled completely beneath the foamy bubbles, the texture of the water slick against her skin, he leaned forward and kissed her until she feared she might drown.

"Here," he said, drying his hand on a towel and then reaching for one of the hair ties she kept in her clear cosmetics bag. "Let me."

With a modicum of splashing, she turned around and settled between his legs. The feel of his erection nestled against the small of her back was invigorating. She couldn't resist scooting closer, pressing against him, reminding herself of his length and thickness.

Though he fumbled a bit, he managed to sweep her thick hair into a ponytail atop her head. "Much better," he said, lowering his mouth to her neck. "Now I can see the delicious flesh I'm nibbling."

The combination of his mouth on her flesh, the sizzling water and the fragrance of lavender made relaxing inevitable. Her entire body surrendered, and her sigh of contentment was utterly honest. Even when his hands drifted across her belly and then up to toy with her breasts, she could hardly move. She was stuck in a state between arousal and peace.

"This is glorious," she said.

He dipped his tongue into the shell of her ear. "You're glorious. I could make love to you for hours on end. Weeks, maybe."

"That would be a first."

"For both of us," he confirmed.

She expected him to tense up. Be defensive about his fickle tastes. Instead, acknowledging his weakness seemed to amuse him.

She found a bath sponge in a basket by the tub, which she dunked into the water. "Doesn't it get tiresome going from woman to woman? I mean, constant change must be exciting, but how can you ever be truly intimate with someone you barely know?"

"You can't," he said, shifting her body so that he could taste the other side of her neck. "That's the whole point, isn't it?"

She squeezed a dollop of bath gel into the sponge and worked up a lather. "Is it?"

He took the soapy ball from her and rubbed it over her arms, neck and shoulders. The sensations were amazing. Together with the feel of his hard chest and erection against her back, his free hand on her legs and breasts, and his accented whisper in her ear, she was cocooned in pleasure.

"What do you know about my family?" he asked.

The question surprised her. "Just what I've read and what Bianca's told me. Your father is a diplomat from the Punjab province of India. Your mother gave birth to you and your twin brother, Raj, in London. You were Oxford-educated until grad school, when you went to MIT."

"I'm a citizen of the world. Indian parents, British upbringing, strong American influences. But though I've never lived in India, my culture has always been important to my family— especially when it came to the expectations on a son."

"You mean marriage?"

"Not just any marriage—a Hindu marriage. Which, to this day, are quite often arranged."

Mallory nodded. She knew from living abroad that marriages set up by the parents of a bride and groom were not at all unheard of—though modern young adults normally had some say in the matter.

"They didn't try to force you to marry anyone, did they?"

"Force?" he asked casually, now focusing the sponge on her leg, which she lifted so he could reach. "I suppose that depends on your definition of the word. They didn't broker any pacts that made me honor-bound to marry, no. But my mother spent a great deal of my adolescence ensuring that I met all the right girls from all the right families. When I finished college, I was expected to choose one and make some random mother-in-law very happy."

"But you didn't," she pointed out.

He chuckled and the rumble of his chest against her back felt nearly as delicious as how he ran the sponge up and down her legs, around her middle and just underneath her breasts. "No, I opted to make myself so unpalatable to any future in-laws that I was safe from the marriage machine."

He chose that moment to rasp the netted ball across her nipples. The soft, yet rough sensation produced an unbidden sigh.

"You're trying to distract me," she said.

His other hand, pressed flat on her belly, slipped downward. "Is it working?"

"You know it is."

"Good, because I think I've reached my limit of personal revelations. Either you tell me something intimate and secret about yourself or turn around and let me kiss you."

Mallory chose the latter. They splashed in the tub, slipping, laughing and kissing until she faced him, her knees on either side of his thighs. She suckled his neck and lower on his chest until she was half-submerged in bubbles.

"Are condoms waterproof?" she asked, reaching across to pluck one from his shaving kit.

"Oh, yeah, but try these." He withdrew a different packet, one that promised extra lubrication.

"I do like a man who is prepared," she said, removing the prophylactic from its pouch. "But I don't think I can put this on while you're...submerged."

They shifted again and when he stood, Mallory's ability to breathe was severely hampered. She watched him dry off his groin area, her mouth watering. He was so incredibly beautiful—from his slim, sculpted chest to his tapered waist and muscled thighs. And his sex, strong and curved, enticed her so powerfully, she could not resist sliding her hands up his legs, balancing on her knees in the bubbles and tasting him.

His skin was sweet and clean and hot from the tub. She licked him, nipped at him, swirled her tongue around the tip of his penis until he tangled his fingers in her hair, his palms cradling her cheeks while she took him into her mouth. The full sensation was invigorating and decadent all at the same time. She sucked him hard, then soft, gauging what he liked best by the sound of his moans and then doing it until she tasted the salty sweet liquid that told her he was close to the edge. She sheathed the condom over him and dragged him back into the water, climbing on top and guiding him inside her.

Her nerve endings were on alert, registering the soft tickle of the bath bubbles, the heat of the water, the completeness of his body inside hers. With her knees on either side of him, she controlled the rhythm of their lovemaking, which she kept slow and steady.

He smeared the bath bubbles over her breasts, then pushed the foam away to bite and lave her nipples until electric sensations rocked her from every direction. He murmured sweet compliments about the beauty of her body, about how perfectly they fit.

"God, Mallory," he said, his voice raspy and hoarse. "You're making me crazy. I just want to come inside you over and over."

She moved lazily, squeezing the pleasure from his body into hers, wanting this afternoon to never, ever end.

Her insides quivered. Her muscles contracted and she felt her control slipping. The edge was within her reach, but if she crossed, this fantasy would be over so soon. And yet, she couldn't resist, especially when he grabbed her hips and forced her down harder and faster. "Yes, Ajay, yes."

Water splashed over the side of the tub. She wrapped her arms around his neck and kissed him hard. The minute their tongues met, her orgasm began. His was soon in sync and by the time they had both come, a tidal wave from the tub had swamped the floor.

She regained her ability to speak just as Ajay grabbed a towel and wiped his face free of water, then did the same for her.

"I guess we're clean," he said.

"Inside and out," she agreed.

She moved to get out of the tub, but he took her hand, kissed it, then stood and wrapped her in a large, dry towel. He tossed the damp one onto the floor to sop up the puddles.

"I don't remember ever making love like this before," he said.

She couldn't control her jaw from dropping in surprise. "All the women you've been with and you've never done it in a bathtub?"

"For the record, I did not sleep with every woman I dated."

She arched a brow. "You want me to believe you haven't had a lot of lovers?"

"No," he said, climbing out of the tub to retrieve a towel to wrap around his waist. "There have been many—too many. But not lately. And to be honest, most of my affairs were forgettable. I don't mean to be insulting to the women, but I didn't want to remember them. Love didn't fit into my master plan."

Didn't?

He'd said *didn't*, not *don't*. Funny how a verb tense threatened to turn her weekend upside down.

Mallory shivered, though she assured herself it was just from the cold air and tepid water swirling around her knees. With his assistance, she stepped out of the tub and dried off. When she sat on the tub's edge to dry her feet, he joined her.

"I just want you to know…I mean, I think I should explain," he said, then stopped. For a man who was famous for always saying exactly the most charming and witty thing, he seemed at a loss for words.

She touched his cheek, and then kissed him softly. "I understand, Ajay," she said, hoping his obvious turmoil would camouflage her own conflicted emotions. "You've made me feel special. I won't forget this weekend. Ever."

With that promise hanging heavily in the air, Mallory forced herself to walk casually out of the room, stopping long enough to throw a saucy look over her shoulder. But once she was out of his sight, she scurried to the bedroom on the other side of the suite and shut the door. Leaning against the cool wood panels, she tried to fight the sudden dizziness that threatened to topple her over.

What had she done?

She was being silly. Ajay's choice of words was accidental. He didn't mean what he'd implied—that a long-term relationship with her might be a possibility. She had not come to him for that. She'd sought him out not only because she found him incredibly attractive, but because he was safe. Good sex. No expectations.

And most importantly, no disappointment.

He'd never had a woman in his life for more than a few nights. He was a world-renowned playboy. A man did not change who he was over the course of one day simply because they were great together in bed—or a bathtub.

And yet, now that he'd told her the reasons behind his choices, she couldn't help but wonder—no matter how she tried—if what she'd thought she'd wanted from him was only part of what they could be.

6

AJAY RAN HIS HAND through his damp hair and cursed under his breath. He watched Mallory stop and throw a sated and satisfied smile over her shoulder, then disappear into her bedroom. She shut the door with a definitive snap. God, how he wanted to go after her, but he was out of juice. She'd worn him out—not just physically, but emotionally.

Which should have been impossible. Unfathomable, even.

Ajay did not get emotionally involved. Ever. Ignoring the sound of the drain sucking down the now cool water, he remained on the edge of the tub, the cold tile biting into his skin as he tried to figure out what the hell had just happened.

On the surface, the facts were simple. A beautiful woman he'd known through mutual friends—a woman he'd done business with for years and that he'd never made a play for—had come to the hotel this morning to seduce him. She'd asked for nothing in return. He'd known that making love to Mallory was a risk, but only because she'd be impossible to avoid in the future. She was Bianca's boss and friend. His company hired hers on a regular basis. But he couldn't resist her. So he'd plunged in, fulfilled her desires and at the same time, a few of his own.

That's where things stopped making sense.

Uninvited and seemingly accidentally, she'd gotten under

his skin. He might have blamed her vulnerability since her breakup, but she seemed resigned to the fact that her former fiancé was now marrying another woman. She hadn't cried or asked his opinion on why Carlo had left her—nor had she called out her ex's name in ecstasy.

It was his name she'd sung out.

Yes, Ajay, yes.

Not exactly poetry, but everything she'd said to him—and everything he'd confessed in return—had struck him deeply. He tried to compare her to the women he'd been with in the past, but Mallory somehow erased every other woman he'd screwed out of his mind.

He couldn't remember faces. He couldn't remember first and last names. He wondered if he'd bothered to call them anything beyond "Baby" or "Honey" or "Darling."

Such wasted time and energy.

He should have held out for someone like Mallory—someone who couldn't imagine having more than a weekend of pleasure with a guy like him, even if he suddenly could imagine nothing less than a lifetime.

Determined to knock some sense back into himself, he got dressed. It was nearly four o'clock. He considered ordering up an early dinner, but decided that staying in the room was not a good idea, so he rang up his favorite restaurant and secured an early reservation. He checked his text messages, dealt with a few business issues, then grabbed his bag and set up his computer. He was just about to try out the prototype flat screen when Mallory emerged from her room.

She'd brushed out her hair and wrapped it into a loose twist. Her makeup, expertly reapplied, drew his attention to her long-lashed, smoky-shadowed eyes. A barely pink gloss shaded her generous lips, making them look sweet enough to eat. She wore a snug pink T-shirt and plush silver tracksuit pants with the word *Juicy* embroidered on her backside. As if her perfect bum needed a label?

"I like your hair that way," he said, picking the safest compliment he could find.

She hummed and touched the twist gingerly. "You're teasing."

"No, I'm not. I don't say things I don't mean."

Her eyes flashed with uncertainty. Maybe even fear. Then she laughed and plopped beside him on the couch. "I wear my hair like this every day, usually secured with a pencil or chopsticks instead of proper hairpins. I think it's kind of schoolmarmish."

A string of sexy comebacks occurred to him, starting with a comment about how it was a time-honored tradition for boys to lust after their teachers, but instead, he returned his gaze to the computer. It wasn't as if he'd seen any hot-to-trot instructors at Eton.

Before he could conjure up a fantasy of Mallory wearing nothing underneath black professor robes, she asked, "What's this?"

She touched the rectangular device sitting beside his laptop.

"This," he said, pressing activation buttons on the corner of his keyboard and the compressed flat screen to sync the devices, "is the newest creation from my R&D department. Coop worked on some of the initial designs. Would you like to see it?"

She nodded and the anticipatory look in her eyes reminded him of how she'd stared at him in the bathtub while he'd stood up to put on the condom—an act she'd interrupted with the most amazing blow job he'd had in a long time. Sex felt so different with her. Was it because he knew her? Because he cared about her?

He cleared his throat, trying not to replay the experience in his mind when he was still trying to recover.

He crossed the room and removed a print hanging on the wall across from the sofa. Determining that the hooks would work adequately, he took the sides of the device in his hands and pulled. The polymers his company had developed stretched to the desired width. He attached the screen to the hooks and then pulled the sides to an adequate length. He stepped back and, satisfied with the shape, went to his computer and keyed in the code to activate his newest invention.

"Oh!"

The screen lit up, an exact mirror of his laptop screen, with impressively crisp quality.

"Cool, yes?"

She stood and examined the device more closely, running her hands gingerly over the edge. When she turned, her mouth was still open in surprise.

"Ajay, this is amazing. Can you adjust it to any size you want?"

He nodded. "It can run small like I had it on the table or slightly larger than what I have now. At least, that's the capability of this version. It can work as a computer screen or a television, in high definition. But you can't tell anyone you've seen it. We're still in the testing stages. We hope to unveil it at the tech shows next year."

"You're going to make a mint," she said, laughing excitedly.

"I already have a mint," he mumbled, but she did not seem to hear his boast as she'd turned back to admire his invention.

He could remember precisely where he was the minute the idea had come to him, when a presentation to investors was foiled by a malfunctioning projection screen. He'd ended up giving his pitch from his laptop. The money men had to shift and stretch to see what he was talking about, and he'd cursed the lack of a custom-designed screen he could take with him easily. If only he could stretch out his own laptop screen…

Yes, he could remember the details behind each and every brainwave he'd ever had, but he couldn't remember the full name of a single lover before Mallory.

What exactly did that say about him?

More than likely, something he did not want to hear.

He pulled up the research he'd accumulated on Brock Arsenal, hoping he'd feel better in comparison.

"According to the latest gossip Web sites, he's not currently seeing anyone," he said.

Mallory grabbed a handful of sweetened almonds the hotel had set out on a china dish. "Might mean he's not in a romantic mood. That certainly won't help our cause. How does he feel about fans?"

Ajay did a search using the term *fans* and the program he'd designed pulled key phrases out of the articles and then displayed the results. Mallory stood in front of the expanded flat screen and read a few out loud.

"Arsenal claims his longevity in the business is due one hundred percent to his fans. 'I'd be retired or singing at a Tiki bar for tips if people did not continue to buy my music and come to my concerts. In the beginning, I never understood the power of the fans. Once you get to be an old fart like me, you start appreciating the people in your life—even the ones you don't personally know.'"

Ajay nodded. "If he really meant what he said, that could work in our favor. I'd never listened to a single Brock Arsenal song until Bianca and Coop introduced me to him."

She looked at him skeptically. "And now you buy all his records?"

He smirked. "Not exactly."

"Let's leave that part out of our pitch."

"Good idea. I think we'll figure out what to say once we meet him. But that's the biggest issue. Just because we're across the hall from him doesn't mean he's going to have a party or that he'll invite us to attend."

Mallory pressed her lips together tightly. "Then let's go back to my original suggestion and have a party ourselves. He can be the guest of honor."

He checked the time on his laptop. "You can pull off a party in less than six hours?"

She shrugged. "Why not? The hotel staff seemed to be tripping over themselves for you downstairs. I'm sure they could plan something in a flash. Just send an e-mail to your employees and tell them to bring dates."

"I don't think a bunch of technology geeks or the women they usually attract are going to catch a rock star's attention."

She returned to the couch. "You're probably right. But you know, I just provided a translator for a group of French dancers and gymnasts that are performing downtown tonight. It's one of those circus-type acts, and from what I've heard, it's very sexy."

She gestured toward his laptop, which he relinquished with pleasure. She scooted closer to him and typed the name of the troupe into the search engine. Seconds later, pictures of lovely, limber ladies flashed onto the screen.

"They should work," he said, trying to stop himself from imagining bending Mallory into similarly provocative poses. Apparently, his expended juices were refilling at lightning speed.

"Let me make a call."

Fifteen minutes later, they had a guest list—a combination of the circus troupe, Ajay's employees and a few VIP guests registered at the hotel. A quarter hour after that, the hotel's entire staff of concierges and event planners had thrown together a menu of canapés, bite-size sweets and liquors perfect for a late-night bash. Now all they needed was to lure the guest of honor. For that, Mallory went downstairs and had a one-on-one conversation with the manager.

She wore her red dress.

"So we're all set?" Ajay asked when she returned.

"Arsenal's plane lands around ten o'clock, and the hotel expects him half an hour later. The manager will invite him to our little soiree upon his arrival. I left a personal note. Even spritzed it with cologne. But the manager suggested we have things going good by that time. If we're loud, Brock'll either join us or call the front desk to have our party shut down."

Ajay frowned. There was a flaw in the plan.

"Did you happen to come up with a reason why we're having this party?" he asked.

"I just said we were celebrating a deal between your company and mine. A merger, of sorts," she said, her voice dipping low as she kicked out of her high heels. "Otherwise, I was sketchy on the details."

"Wasn't exactly a lie," he said, holding his hand out to her.

He couldn't resist. He'd gone way too long without touching her. If he did not take her into his arms very soon, he might lose his mind. He'd never experienced anyone as addicting as Mallory. Trouble was, the sooner they brought Arsenal on board for the reception, the sooner she might leave.

She slipped her palm into his hand and allowed him to reel her onto his lap. He kissed her deeply and only several moments later did he realize he was attempting to memorize the shape of her mouth, the hollow of her throat, the dip between her breasts.

"Ajay, we're going to be late for dinner."

"I'm not hungry," he said.

"Could have fooled me," she replied with a chuckle.

Her eyes flashed with humor as she gave him a gentle push that broadcasted her decision not to give in this time. Had she been this sure of herself this morning? This bold and in control? What about before, when they were merely business associates and shared mutual friends? Had that been the real reason why he'd never pursued her? Because unlike his previous conquests, she actually had the strength and confidence to tell him no?

"I'm going to change," she said, sliding off his lap. She paused for a second and her teeth snagged her bottom lip.

He tensed. Her eyes darkened with what resembled a twinge of sadness before she pasted on a smile and continued, "We can stop downstairs on our way out and make sure everything's all set. If we're lucky, we'll have our project successfully completed by midnight."

Without a backward glance this time, she scurried into her room and shut the door.

Ajay's corporate success had, from the first day, hinged on the idiom that "necessity was the mother of invention." When he needed a device that did not exist, he created it. Right now, he would have given his right hand for a toy that would allow him to read Mallory's mind.

Barring that, he'd simply have to find another way to convince her that his past was just that—his past. He wanted her, and not just for the weekend. He could not say how long they would last, he had no experience in that arena. But the thought of not touching her again, not feeling her lips on his skin, not hearing her voice or her throaty laughter tore at his insides.

He had to convince her that he was worth chancing her heart over—and he had less than five hours to do it.

7

DINNER WAS SPECTACULAR. Ajay had pulled out all the stops, starting with a limousine that delivered them to his favorite restaurant, where he fed her oysters on the half shell, a beautiful salad topped with sweet berries and artisan cheeses, and a main course of seared scallops on a bed of crisp vegetables. Since they were serving a smorgasbord of desserts at the party tonight, they opted to end their meal with brandy and lightly sugared madeleine cookies, served on a settee in front of a fireplace in the restaurant's dark, paneled lounge.

People mingled all around them, yet Mallory never felt their presence intruding. In fact, as Ajay detailed a hilarious story about him and his twin switching places before an important biology exam, she could imagine they were entirely alone rather than in a popular culinary hotspot. Ajay had been nothing short of attentive, barely giving anyone else in the room a second glance. Gazing into his eyes, she could see no one reflected there but herself.

"And so we had detention for the rest of the school year and the headmaster decided he needed a foolproof way to tell us apart. My father suggested tattoos."

Mallory laughed. "I think the pain factor might have played into his idea."

"Most definitely," he replied, snickering. "Luckily, tattoos weren't exactly part of the dress code. He opted to shave Raj's head."

"He didn't!"

Ajay's expression was one of utter mirth. "He did."

"And you got away scot-free?"

"Well, the whole mess was Raj's idea," he argued. "I was always better in science, which is frightening since he's now a doctor. But the headmaster was no fool. He ordered me to alter my uniform a bit. Instead of my own starched shirts, I wore a few that had accidentally mixed with a red football sock in the wash."

She laughed at the idea of Ajay walking around in a pink shirt in such a serious academic atmosphere. But he seemed to remember the whole situation fondly. He'd told a lot of stories about growing up in London, traveling with his diplomat father, experiencing culture shock when he'd returned to India for prolonged stays with his grandparents.

Surprisingly, she'd shared just as much, describing her parents' whirlwind romance in the Philippines just before the American military base closed and how her Irish-Italian father had shocked his relatives back home by marrying a local girl, and opting not to renew his commission in order to run a small hotel on Boracay Beach, where Mallory had honed her language skills on the tourists.

They'd talked about so many topics—except one.

"Are you ready to head back?" he asked, slipping his credit card to the waiter who had just appeared with their bill.

"No," she answered honestly, leaning back against his shoulder while she sipped her liqueur. "I could stay here forever."

"We can come again," he offered.

"Tomorrow night is when Leo announces the surprise ceremony to Bianca and Coop," she pointed out. "And Sunday night is the wedding."

"The wedding doesn't have to be our endgame, Mallory," he said.

Her chest clenched. "Doesn't it?"

"No, it doesn't."

She shifted to the side so she could look into his eyes. He leaned forward, his elbows on his knees, his jade-green gaze sparkling with sincerity.

"You've never had a real relationship, Ajay. And I can't afford to be hurt again. Can't we just enjoy the moment? Live for the now? Then go our separate ways after the wedding with no hearts broken?"

He groaned, but the emotion wasn't targeted at her, but at himself. "I wish I could say my reputation is exaggerated, but my past doesn't change that I want to spend more time with you. I admit, up until now I've made it a rule to keep my…interactions…with women brief. I can't even call them relationships. They were just, I don't know—"

"Flings?" she provided.

"Yeah," he confirmed. "As long as I refused to get serious when it came to my personal life, my family and the matchmakers left me alone. No one offered me up to the daughter of their best friend or second cousin, three times removed."

"You know, not that I'm judging you, but that's a pretty pathetic way to avoid commitment." She downed the last of her brandy and waited while he signed the sales slip.

"I've figured that much out now," he replied. "Thanks in part to you."

Ajay stood and with his hand on the small of her back, guided Mallory through the busy restaurant. She had not noticed how crowded the place had become. For an instant, her equilibrium shifted. Her body temperature suddenly soared and the inside of her throat constricted enough to make breathing difficult. Torn between the instinct to freeze or make a quick dash to the exit, she hesitated until Ajay wrapped his arm protectively around her.

"We're only a few feet away from the door. Just focus on me."

She nodded and as promised, they were outside in the sultry Florida night before she knew it. He gave her time to inhale the moss-scented air with measured breaths. Out of the corner of her eye, she watched him gesture for the limousine. A few minutes later, they were cocooned in the safety of the spacious backseat.

"Enochlophobia?" he asked.

Geez, was there anything the man didn't know?

He smiled at what must have been her shocked expression. "When I'm not having one-night stands with nameless women, I read a lot."

The self-deprecating comment broke the tension that had begun to build when they'd discussed his past. He certainly seemed to always know the exact right thing to do since they'd been together. He'd missed no opportunity to impress her, from hot sex in a decadent bubble bath to strawberries, champagne and oysters. He'd hit every cliché in the great seducer's handbook, but somehow, each gesture had felt fresh and new—as if he were the first man on Earth to attempt to entice a woman with such care and attention.

Only, he hadn't needed to entice her, had he? She'd come to the hotel today not only ready, willing and able, but determined to have him. They'd both succeeded in their missions, and yet, why did she feel so...incomplete?

"Fearing crowds has to be hard on a woman who's lived in both Hong Kong and New Delhi," he said.

"It didn't hit me until I started traveling. I grew up in my parents' hotel, but we were on a small island and we never had more than twenty guests at a time. I was always pretty outgoing. But the minute I ventured out into the world...well, I've learned to manage."

"Is that why you never went clubbing with Carlo?"

"That was my excuse, yeah, but I just went to an overflowing restaurant with you and I didn't even notice until the end of the night."

"Must be the company," he said, winking.

Her insides fluttered. "Must be. I had a really nice time tonight, Ajay, and I'm looking forward to the rest of the weekend, but you don't have to change who you are because of me. I'm okay with this just being a fling."

He frowned. "What if I'm not?"

"You've been okay with it for every other woman you've made love to. Why not me?"

"Maybe you've changed me," he claimed.

She laughed, but this only caused him to scowl more deeply.

"Ajay, I didn't mean—"

He cut her off, and she was actually glad. She wasn't sure what to say. He'd seemed utterly at ease with his reputation and mode of living earlier. She couldn't fathom why it was bothering him now.

"Yes, you did mean it. The concept of a person changing overnight is absurd. But I can't lie about what I feel when I'm with you. I've never had much of a so-called love life. Love was never an issue. And before you came along, I didn't take notice."

"I didn't intend to judge you, Ajay."

"Didn't you?" he asked, and his tone held not accusation, but resignation. "You were feeling low about yourself after that idiot dumped you. So who did you pick to get you out of that funk? The guy who'll screw anyone."

She gasped. "That's disgusting."

"But true."

"No, it's not true. You only slept with worldly women, fun women, women who lived the same high-flying lifestyle you did. Women you wouldn't hurt when you walked away. But your past wasn't the only reason I was attracted to you. You're handsome and smart and, yes, sexual. You're a man who enjoys pleasure. You love life and live to make love."

Even she could hear the wistfulness in her voice, the want. Being with Ajay today, casting off her fears and plunging into an affair, had reinvigorated her. If she believed for one moment that she and Ajay could experience this for the long run, she'd grab the chance. But Ajay didn't do long run—and she wasn't entirely sure she could, either.

"I envied that in you," she confessed. "And yes, I wanted to be a part of it, if only for a weekend. In the process, I've learned you're more than your reputation, and to be honest, I guess I do wish that we could stretch this out beyond the weekend. But I can't set myself up for disappointment. I'm just getting over being hurt. I can't take that risk again."

He took her hands and placed one light kiss atop each.

"I wish I could make bigger promises," he said.

"I'm just glad you live up to the ones you do make."

"Have I promised to see to it that your next orgasm lasts at least a half hour?" he said, grinning.

"That's impossible."

"Wrong thing to say to a man who believes anything is possible, if he puts his mind to it."

THE LIMO DRIVER had to make an extra few turns around the neighborhood, but by the time they finally arrived at the hotel thirty minutes later, Ajay had made good on his pledge. And though he'd slipped on a condom and finished the job with a bang, he knew sex alone wouldn't convince Mallory that he wanted more. For her and for him.

He could not hand her any guarantees. No man could, especially one so inexperienced in the area of relationships. But damn it, he wanted to try.

With Mallory.

He instructed the driver to park in the hotel's side lot, which was dark with the shadows of old oak trees, and then sent him into the hotel to check on the preparations for the party. This not only gave Ajay a chance to clear up and straighten his clothes, but Mallory time to put herself back together. Making her come undone was addicting, but they did have a goal to achieve. Hopefully, they'd shore up Brock Arsenal's performance quickly so he could throw out everyone he'd invited for the party and he could spend the rest of the night proving to her that he wouldn't lose interest in making her happy.

When she finally exited the car, he pulled her close and twirled his finger around a tendril of hair that had escaped her chic French twist. "Your cheeks are flushed."

"That's not the only part of me that's flushed," she said.

"Oh, can I see?"

She slapped him lightly on the shoulder. "You had a bird's-eye view only fifteen minutes ago. That's a wicked tongue you have."

"I'm glad you appreciate my talents."

"Yes, well, if I don't stop appreciating your talents, I'm going to have to redo my makeup for a third time. We should greet our guests. Do you think Arsenal will show up, or will we have to turn up the music really loud and hope he comes over personally to complain?"

"We issued the invitation," Ajay said. "Now all we can do is hope the music and those Parisian gymnasts do the rest."

In the penthouse, waitstaff passed out savory appetizers, bite-size desserts and flutes of champagne. Ajay's team was there in force, some with girlfriends and wives, but most anxiously waiting for the performers to arrive. Two of Mallory's translators came in ten minutes later, followed by the contingent from the circus.

He usually enjoyed parties, meeting new people, even catching up with the designers and technicians he'd hired but rarely had time to socialize with. He ran a relatively laid-back company, but everyone was too in love with their work to goof off. But by the time the disc jockey had Brock Arsenal's most popular songs rocking the entire upper floor of the hotel, Ajay wanted to get this over with.

Mallory stuck close to him, more so as the crowd increased with guests from the hotel. If they got separated by the swelling sea of people, including a few strange faces he suspected were gate-crashers, he instinctively found her, taking her hand and locking it in his or pressing his palm against her back so that she was constantly aware of his presence.

As midnight approached with no appearance from their unwitting guest of honor, Ajay felt Mallory's skin chill. He pulled her close, but her breathing had quickened more than necessary for someone who was just working a room.

"Why don't we step outside for some fresh air?" he suggested, gesturing with his champagne toward the balcony.

"We might miss Arsenal if he comes in."

"Then let's go out into the hall. We could both use a few quiet moments."

"Are you going to kiss my lipstick off again?" she asked, leaning up to mouth the question directly into his ear.

"Now that you suggested it, yes."

8

Ajay's KISS sucked all the pent-up anxiety out of her system. He was like a panacea. Or a drug. Mallory had never understood the true power of addiction until he'd come into her life.

And he wanted more. How could she deny him? She was pretty sure no one had yet devised a twelve-step program to stop this kind of madness.

A deep-throated *Ahem* broke them apart.

Their neighbor and quarry stared at them, completely unabashed.

"Mr. Arsenal," she sputtered.

Brock Arsenal looked every inch the rock star. His blond hair, highlighted with streaks of gray, shot from his head in spikes. His lined face bore signs of his wild life, but his blue eyes danced with humor. He slid the tops of his fingers into the pockets of tight denim jeans and his hips moved almost imperceptibly, picking up the beat of the one of his hits that had been remixed into a dance club staple.

"And here I thought the party was inside," he said, his New Jersey accent only barely hidden by his chuckle.

Ajay stepped forward and extended his hand. At the moment, Mallory was more than ready for him to take over, but she suddenly realized that meeting Brock Arsenal was the first step toward the end of this marvelous, liberating affair.

But she couldn't stop time. Whether this rock star sang at the reception or not, in two days, her best friend was going to marry the love of her life—and after that, Mallory would have to pull away from Ajay, a man who had, in less than twenty-four hours, touched her in places her former fiancé never knew existed. Physically and emotionally.

Damn him.

"We just stepped out for some fresh air," Ajay explained.

Arsenal leaned toward Mallory's face and inhaled. "Yes, that's some minty fresh air. And beautiful lips to breathe it with. Brock Arsenal," he said, holding out his hand. "And who might this delicious provider of oxygen be?"

Oh, Lord. He was flirting with her. She nearly shot off a comment that would have made it clear she wasn't interested—but Ajay, who was still holding her hand, gave it an anxious squeeze.

Right. If she was rude, they might not get the guy's co-operation.

She pasted on a smile. "Mallory Tedesco. And this is Ajay Singh. We're hosting tonight's event."

"Singh? Popular name. You're not the golfer, are you?"

"That's Vijay Singh. And no, we're not related."

Arsenal grinned and from the wicked look in his eye, Mallory guessed his incorrect assumption about Ajay's identity was a joke.

"Then that makes you the tech guy. I think your company designed the software that runs the light sequences for my live show."

Ajay's brows arched. "I don't recall—"

"Oh, they weren't custom. My team adapted the equipment from The Magics. Their lead singer got all coked out and the group broke up. Someone put their junk up for auction and I bought it for a steal."

Ajay grinned. "Well, we'll have to develop something more state-of-the-art for you. If you'd like to come inside, meet a few people, we can discuss your current needs."

"Nah," the rock star said. "Just wanted to thank you for the invite. Sounds like a hot get-together. Music rocks, anyway. But I've got someplace I've got to be."

"You must have a very busy weekend," Mallory said quickly, desperate to keep the man talking. If he wasn't going to stay for the party, they had to work fast to make their proposal. "Your concert is tomorrow night."

"Yeah," he said. "You got tickets?"

"Front row," Ajay replied. "But I'm not sure if we're going to be able to use them. Two friends of ours are flying in from Costa Rica and tomorrow night, we have the rehearsal for their wedding on Sunday. Your ballad, 'Forever Mine,' is their song."

"Cool," he said, nodding. "Who doesn't like weddings?"

Mallory swooped in, stepping forward in her eagerness to grab this opening. "You'd really like this one. They've been engaged for ten years but haven't managed to get down the aisle, so we're throwing them a wedding as a surprise. They have no idea we've made all the arrangements. Well, most of the arrangements. We have one last miracle to pull off."

Together, Ajay and Mallory described Bianca and Coop's romance, highlighting their tribulations, their amazing, giving personalities and their long road toward matrimony. Arsenal tilted his head as he listened. His body language—something Mallory wasn't exactly fluent in, though she knew the basics— told her he was genuinely interested.

"Man, romances like that just don't happen anymore," he said, shaking his head.

"But when they do," Ajay said, slipping his arm around Mallory's waist and pulling her close, "don't you think the couple should just go for it? Do it up big?"

"Don't ask me. I'm crap at relationships. Although," he said, glancing at his watch, "I never stop trying."

He had a date. Or in his case, probably a rendezvous. It was time to drop all pretenses.

"Are you going to be around all weekend? Because Coop and Bianca would go crazy if you came to the wedding! Oh, my God. That would be like a blessing from the musician who created the soundtrack of their love."

Arsenal's brow arched. She'd caught his attention.

"I could make it worth your time," Ajay added, giving Mallory an expectant squeeze on her backside that the rock star could not see, "A large donation to your favorite charity, perhaps? I know you're on tour, but—"

"Hey," Arsenal said, stopping Ajay with a flat palm on his arm. "The best part of being in this business for more than half my life is that I make my own rules. No entourage in my private room, no rush in my schedule. I'd planned to spend the whole weekend here, actually. Was just going to head to the beach Sunday and bum around. But going to a wedding could be cool. And if you want to put a little cash in the coffers of this animal shelter I'm supporting in upstate New York, then more power to you, man."

In minutes, the details were exchanged and verified. Hands were shaken. Hugs commenced. By the time the rock star headed down the elevator, Mallory's mind was whirling.

"We did it," she squealed.

Ajay scooped her into his arms. All the anxiety she'd felt earlier in the overcrowded suite had evaporated and the euphoria of achieving their goal had her floating on air. Or perhaps the lightness came from Ajay twirling her in circles and kissing her until she couldn't breathe.

"Now," Ajay said finally, setting her down and piercing her with a gaze so serious her heart skipped a beat, "let's kick all these people out of here. Until tomorrow night we have nothing left to do except make love until neither one of us can stand."

A thrill skittered through her bloodstream. Mallory had never heard such an irresistible offer—one she would never dream of refusing. And if he kept this up, she could only imagine what else she might agree to.

As PROMISED, Mallory and Ajay spent the rest of the night and most of Saturday lounging in the suite, ordering room service and making love whenever the mood struck them. By the time they reached the wedding rehearsal just before Bianca and Coop, neither had much energy. Mallory felt as if she'd just touched down after a trip in a time machine—one where she'd shoved a lifetime's worth of loving into one twenty-four-hour period.

Afterward, they walked into the pizzeria, the same spot where Mallory had first set her sights on Ajay, hand in hand. Their pairing hadn't raised even the tiniest eyebrow from anyone. The shock of Jessie and Leo's reconciliation, not to mention the pure disbelief over the unexpected pairing of Coop's sister, Annie, and Bianca's much younger brother, Drew, won the moment. Even the announcement that the group had banded together to throw Coop and Bianca a surprise wedding that would happen the next night had not trumped the collective disbelief over the unexpected romances.

Since no one seemed to care about them, Mallory was able to throw herself completely into the role of Ajay's lover. Surrounded by people she cared about, the excessive crowd in the busy Saturday-night hot spot didn't affect her at all. She and Ajay held hands under the table, kissed when no one was looking, shared pasta-twirled forks and talked in hushed tones. By the time they returned to the hotel, they walked in as if the rooms were their shared home rather than a rented suite, discarded their clothes, showered together and then fell into bed. They did not make love, but slept entangled in each other's arms until late the next morning.

From the moment they woke, however, the wedding became their priority. Ajay shuttled Mallory to the hotel where the wedding would be held and picked up Coop, Drew and Leo so they could use Ajay's suite to don their tuxedos and spend the afternoon drinking cold imported beer and enjoying the last moments of Coop's bachelorhood.

Not that he'd been a bachelor for a long time. For a decade, his devotion to Bianca had never hinged on a ring or a piece of paper. The wedding was just an excuse to celebrate a relationship that each and every one of them knew would last a lifetime.

When Bianca came out of her bedroom in her custom-designed wedding dress, Mallory allowed herself a full minute of pure and utter envy before she joined the queue to hug her friend and wish her the best life had to offer.

"You've never looked more beautiful," Mallory said, wiping away a tear that threatened her expertly applied mascara.

"You look amazing yourself," Bianca said. "Love looks good on you."

"Love?"

Bianca smirked. "Don't deny it. I'm a bride. We know these things."

Mallory opened her mouth to offer a reasoned argument about why she could not possibly be in love with a man she barely knew—not to mention one with no concept of commitment—but she stopped. She was never a good liar. She might be adept at deluding herself, but even that talent was pretty weak, judging by the way she'd forgotten all about her so-called heartbreak over Carlo after only two days as Ajay's lover.

"He's going to leave me," she said.

"No, he won't," Bianca assured, turning to the mirror to adjust the antique tiara her mother had unveiled shortly after their arrival at the hotel.

Jessie and Annie sat near the window as makeup artists finished the last touches on their lipstick. Bianca's mother had gone downstairs for one last meeting with the caterer, and the photographer was lingering by the kitchen, noshing on crudités left out for the bridal party. Mallory was glad for this private moment with Bianca, but did she want to waste it discussing something that couldn't possibly be true?

"How can you say that? You're the one who warned me off spending the weekend with him."

"I guess it's my superhoned bride-sense," Bianca joked. She laughed, but then her expression turned serious. "Because I saw the two of you together last night. I've seen Ajay with lots of women and he never looked at any of them like that."

"With lust?" Mallory challenged.

"Well, there was a load of that going around the whole

table, if you ask me," Bianca said, eying Jessie and Annie with a perplexed gaze. "But it was more than lust. He looked at you the way Coop looks at me. I've never seen it in Ajay. I'm surprised you kept from ripping his clothes off every time you caught him staring."

This time, Mallory laughed. "Trust me, we've both been naked more often than not this weekend."

Jessie jumped up from her chair with a glare at the makeup artist that declared she'd had enough primping. "Sounds like we all shared the surprise wedding aphrodisiac this weekend."

Annie went to the mirror on the other side of the room and pretended to mess with her perfectly coiffed hair. Bianca caught her by the arm and dragged her back over. "Oh, no. You're not getting out of this conversation."

The mother of two quelled the bride's curiosity with one deadpan look and a loaded question. "Do you really want to know about your brother's lovemaking techniques?"

Bianca grimaced and let her go. "You're right. You stay out of this. Except you're the only one of us who's ever been married before. Why don't you tell Mallory how to make sure Ajay never strays?"

Annie choked. "Like I know? Look, there are no guarantees in life or love, but if there's one thing I have learned, especially this weekend with Drew, it's that I need to be true to myself. We all do. If Ajay loves you for who you are now, at this very moment, and for whoever you might become over the course of your life—and you love him the same way—then nothing can come between you."

Mallory mulled over Annie's wisdom, and she had to admit the woman had a point. Ajay was utterly comfortable in his own skin. His confidence gave her room to be whoever she wanted to be—and vice versa. Ajay knew his weaknesses. He admitted them freely. But he also knew his strengths. So far, he'd never failed at anything he'd put his mind to. Why would he fall short now?

"Go for it," Bianca said. "Take a risk. You already have just by hooking up with him and so far, you've come out the better for it. Maybe Ajay never committed to anyone because he hadn't met the right woman. Now he's met you. Game over."

The late afternoon ceremony went on without a hitch, though the fact that Brock Arsenal came into the ballroom with the groomsmen caused a stir, which was silenced immediately once the bridesmaids started the procession down the long white runner. Once Bianca and Coop exchanged vows and kissed, the wedding guests retreated to a larger ballroom and partook of appetizers and cocktails while the bridal party posed for picture after picture after picture.

Bianca insisted on separate shots of each of her attendants and the men in their lives. When the photographer posed Mallory and Ajay in profile, each looking deeply into the other's eyes, Mallory's fears disappeared. She could see his love there as plainly as she could see the tiny flecks of light in his jade-green irises. She could feel it in the way he held her, possessively, and yet, with total confidence that once he let her go, she'd gravitate right back to him.

And she would. They were two pieces of one whole.

She wanted Ajay more than she'd ever wanted anything else, and not just for the weekend, but for a lifetime. She'd come so far in such a short time—she knew that if she concentrated on her goal, she'd have him forever.

Mind, body and soul.

Brock Arsenal took to the stage and sang his ballad to the bride and groom as they danced for the first time as husband and wife. After the second verse, he called the rest of the bridal party to the dance floor. Mallory took a moment to watch Leo swing Jessie in a crazy circle around the room, while Drew dipped and twirled Annie as if he were channeling Fred Astaire. She and Ajay, however, merely swayed. He had her hand clasped in his and pressed tight against his chest.

"This can't be the end, Mallory," he said.

"I know," she said.

"You have to give me a chance to—what?"

She smiled. His eyes had widened and he stopped moving.

"I said 'I know.' I don't want it to end. I want you, Ajay. I love you."

She'd expected a long silence, a pregnant pause while he processed her confession, but his reaction was immediate. He slipped his hands down her bottom and lifted her, spinning her as he kissed her in front of everyone in the room.

When he finally set her down, Mallory expected the attention to trigger her phobia, but Ajay kept her gaze focused on him while he whispered words she'd never in her life imagined he'd say.

"Mallory, I love you, too. If you promise to marry me, I'll be the richest man in the universe."

"Marry you? But we've only been together for two days!"

Ajay's devoted expression didn't waver. "My parents only knew each other for a day before they married. My grandparents only an hour. And yet, they're all still together. I've run from commitment my whole life. I'm done. If you'll have me, I'm yours forever."

Mallory could barely speak, but she breathed deeply and finally managed to utter the most important word she'd ever speak in any language.

"Yes."

Epilogue

AFTER FOUR HOURS of talking, eating, drinking and kissing on command every time someone at the reception clinked their glass with their fork, Bianca squealed with delight when Coop danced her into a corner, twirled her behind a lighted palm tree and proceeded to kiss her senseless. Over the course of the day, she'd kissed her new husband more times than she could count—and each time, she recognized how different his mouth felt on hers.

She couldn't accurately describe the sensation, but if she had to give it her best guess, she'd declare that when they were only engaged, their kisses spoke of needfulness. Now, the joining of their mouths represented the ultimate combining of their spirits.

She still wanted Coop with raw desire, but needing him was no longer necessary—he would always be with her. In her heart. In her mind. In her soul.

They slipped onto a deserted balcony overlooking the Hillsborough River. Coop shut the curtained glass door firmly, then put a chair in front of the handle to guarantee them more than a few seconds alone.

"Mrs. Rush," he said, taking both her hands and tugging her close.

"Mr. Rush," she replied, kissing along the ridge of his chin. "Or are you keeping Brighton? We've never discussed it."

"I don't care," she said honestly. "Do you?"

"All I care about is you, beautiful. I can't believe our friends pulled off a surprise wedding. I can't believe Leo and Jessie are back together."

"Apparently, weddings make everything possible."

She sounded giddy and dreamy and girly and silly and she loved it. Life couldn't be more perfect than at this very moment. She had the man of her dreams in her arms; the night was cool and clear. In the morning, they'd set off to the private island in the Keys where they'd first traveled together with no expectations or responsibilities beyond enjoying each other.

"I'm not so sure about Annie and Drew, though," Coop complained.

She was nibbling on his neck, so she sensed his scowl more than saw it.

"Lighten up," she chastised. "Annie's a big girl. She doesn't need her brother or anyone else dictating her life to her. You know Drew, and my brother is the real deal. He would never hurt Annie or the boys."

He grumbled for a split second more, until he realized she was loosening the waistband of his tuxedo. Then his growls turned to groans of pleasure, which emboldened her all the more. She and Coop could not be the only bride and groom in the history of weddings to sneak off and enjoy their marital rights slightly before the official start of the honeymoon.

But before she could slip her hands into his pants, he asked, "And what about Mallory and Ajay? He already called his mother. Our next trip will likely be to India for their wedding, and they've only been together for two days."

Bianca chuckled, then took him in her hand, loving how quickly his body responded to her touch. "Not everyone has to wait ten years, Mr. Rush."

He kissed her as he scrunched her skirt up to her waist and flicked aside the wispy material of her satin lingerie. "I'd say you were worth the wait, Mrs. Rush. Wouldn't you say the same?"

Actually, she couldn't say much of anything. Before she

could form an answer, Coop pressed inside her. On a quiet balcony with only the stars to witness their first time making love as husband and wife, Bianca and Coop clung to each other, pleasured each other and loved each other with the passion that had sustained them for a decade and would, without a doubt, keep them together for the rest of their lives.

* * * * *

Want to know about Bianca and Coop's
romantic adventure in Costa Rica?
Check out the free online read by Julie Leto
at www.eHarlequin.com!

COMING NEXT MONTH

Available June 29, 2010

#549 BORN ON THE 4TH OF JULY
Jill Shalvis, Rhonda Nelson, Karen Foley

#550 AMBUSHED!
Vicki Lewis Thompson
Sons of Chance

#551 THE BRADDOCK BOYS: BRENT
Kimberly Raye
Love at First Bite

#552 THE TUTOR
Hope Tarr
Blaze Historicals

#553 MY FAKE FIANCÉE
Nancy Warren
Forbidden Fantasies

#554 SIMON SAYS...
Donna Kauffman
The Wrong Bed

HBCNM0610

REQUEST YOUR FREE BOOKS!

2 FREE NOVELS
PLUS 2
FREE GIFTS!

HARLEQUIN®

Blaze

Red-hot reads!

HARLEQUIN®

A Romance

FOR EVERY MOOD™

Spotlight on
Heart & Home

Heartwarming romances
where love can happen
right when you least expect it.

See the next page to enjoy a sneak peek
from Silhouette Special Edition®,
a Heart and Home series.

*Introducing McFARLANE'S PERFECT BRIDE
by USA TODAY bestselling author Christine Rimmer,
from Silhouette Special Edition®.*

Entranced. Captivated. Enchanted.

Connor sat across the table from Tori Jones and
couldn't help thinking that those words exactly described
what effect the small-town schoolteacher had on him.
He might as well stop trying to tell himself he wasn't
interested. He was powerfully drawn to her.

Clearly, he should have dated more when he was
younger.

There had been a couple of other women since Jennifer
had walked out on him. But he had never been entranced.
Or captivated. Or enchanted.

Until now.

He wanted her—*her,* Tori Jones, in particular. Not just
someone suitably attractive and well-bred, as Jennifer had
been. Not just someone sophisticated, sexually exciting
and discreet, which pretty much described the two women
he'd dated after his marriage crashed and burned.

It came to him that he…he *liked* this woman. And that
was new to him. He liked her quick wit, her wisdom and
her big heart. He liked the passion in her voice when she
talked about things she believed in.

He liked *her.* And suddenly it mattered all out of
proportion that she might like him, too.

Was he losing it? He couldn't help but wonder. Was
he cracking under the strain—of the soured economy, the
McFarlane House setbacks, his divorce, the scary changes
in his son? Of the changes he'd decided he needed to make
in his life and himself?

Strangely, right then, on his first date with Tori Jones, he didn't care if he just might be going over the edge. He was having a great time—having *fun,* of all things—and he didn't want it to end.

Is Connor finally able to admit his feelings to Tori, and are they reciprocated?
Find out in McFARLANE'S PERFECT BRIDE
by USA TODAY bestselling author Christine Rimmer.
Available July 2010,
only from Silhouette Special Edition®.

HARLEQUIN *Presents*

Bestselling Harlequin Presents® author

Penny Jordan

brings you an exciting new trilogy…

Needed:
THE WORLD'S MOST
ELIGIBLE
BILLIONAIRES

Three penniless sisters:
how far will they go to save the ones they love?

Lizzie, Charley and Ruby refuse to drown in their debts.
And three of the richest, most ruthless men in the world
are about to enter their lives. Pure, proud but penniless,
how far will these sisters go to save the ones they love?

Look out for

Lizzie's story—THE WEALTHY GREEK'S
CONTRACT WIFE, July

Charley's story—THE ITALIAN DUKE'S
VIRGIN MISTRESS, August

Ruby's story—MARRIAGE: TO CLAIM HIS TWINS,
September

www.eHarlequin.com

HP12927

Silhouette *Desire*

USA TODAY bestselling author

MAUREEN CHILD

brings you the first
of a six-book miniseries—

Dynasties: The Jarrods

Book one:

CLAIMING HER BILLION-DOLLAR BIRTHRIGHT

Erica Prentice has set out to claim
her billion-dollar inheritance
and the man she loves.

*Available in July
wherever you buy books.*

Always Powerful, Passionate and Provocative.